the Mystic Market

Ruth Perkinson

Bella
BOOKS

2011

Bella Books, Inc.
P.O. Box 10543
Tallahassee, FL 32302

Printed in the United States of America on acid-free paper
First published 2011

Editor: Katherine V. Forrest
Cover Designer: Kiaro Creative

ISBN 13: 978-1-59493-256-4

PUBLISHER'S NOTE

Other Bella books by Ruth Perkinson

Sterling Road Blues

Other Spinsters Ink titles

Breaking Spirit Bridge

Piper's Someday

Vera's Still Point

For Heather

Acknowledgments

Thanks to Lee St. Marie and her sister, Suzanne, who read the first draft and gave me the enthusiastic response writers need to carry on. I can always count on them to give me sound support. Also, a special shout out to Beth Panilaitis, the executive director of ROSMY in Richmond, Virginia. She led me in the right direction when I had several legal questions and is raising the bar for LGBTQ youth everywhere. PFLAG in Jackson Hole answered my questions with warmth and open arms. Lovely.

Katherine V. Forrest truly molded this one as some of the scenes needed some fleshing in and some fleshing out. When her hands and mind edit my writing, it always makes it better. A gift.

Thanks to Linda Hill for number five.

For my mother, my father, my sister, and my brother and my uncle Ron and his family. That move to Jackson Hole in 1976 made an indelible memory. Our journey in this life has proven quite magical. Thank you for your support in light of all the challenges that have been speed bumps along my way.

Thanks to Diana Fleming who considers me a part of her wonderful family and also to her sister, Bonnie, who I hope will one day believe that anything is possible with all the love in the world. She has the best daughter on the planet.

Finally, thank you for the readers who read my work all over this nation and this planet. I never thought I'd live one more day to write these things. But the spirit in you touches the spirit in me. Thank you.

All my love to you, your animals, and your families.

Ruth and River (my shepherd mix), 2011

About The Author

Ruth Perkinson lives in Richmond, Virginia with her dog, River. She is the author of *Vera's Still Point, Piper's Someday,* and *Breaking Spirit Bridge*. She is currently working on her fifth novel. You can read more about her at www.ruthperkinson.net.

CHAPTER ONE

Growing up on Hansen Street in the small tourist town of Jackson Hole, Wyoming, I learned quickly to question priests, politicians and prayer. Prayers especially because, even though I recited many and fumbled with the knots on a mail-order rosary, I found they did not work.

For me, it was terribly personal combined with a generous supply of the common hurts and hindrances: bloody noses, failing tests on fractions, monsters behind my closet door—an occasional spanking to yield better results in cleaning my room, paying attention, and not saying "Go to Hell!" to my brother. Then at night, when I was feeling less sorry for myself, I thought of the whole world and the inordinate amount of head-turning by God to the poor, the dejected, the afflicted, and the tortured. The American debt I didn't understand, nor the starving children in Africa, the polar bears swimming in vain to make it to the next iceberg. I placed a pillow over my head and asked, why?

Simple enough. Why?

After several years of half smothering myself, one Sunday during a scripture reading of Luke, an unexpected answer struck me directly in the head and heart. I heard the priest read the gobbledy-gook I did not understand till he got to the part where it said, *"Even the hairs of your head have all been counted."* It was a perfect solution to the *why*. I'd been staring at the back of Carleen Proust's head and neck when the words emerged. He's distracted with the counting of our hairs? I thought. Hair. Yes, hair. Perfect solution. The Alpha and Omega at the corner hair salon of the universe doing hair like a paint by numbers. Then in my small inconsequential childlike mind, I thought, does he count our leg hairs, too? Or just the tops of us all including the likes of Osama bin Laden or George Bush or Muammar Gaddafi or Fred Phelps? I'd read the newspaper for clues to how these people got away with hate and murder. Did Hitler's head get counted twice or Mussolini's, perhaps Stalin's? I bet he got slowed up with counting the hairs on their chinny chin chins. Our God, God love him, is apparently mired in the infinitesimal details with endless creations to count.

Scripture says he counts hair. God, apparently, has OCD. I might have been wrong but it certainly sounded so.

He must be completely lost in his own affliction.

But, I guess people pray anyway. Like the mystical women at the market where my bungalow houses me and my paralyzed brother, Aaron. I was sure God was counting bricks in the Great Wall of China the day Aaron was born. Or perhaps He was counting miracles and men smoking cigars and whacking each other on their respective backs as if their small sperm had ridden on saddled cowboy cannonballs to the womb creating what they did in the three-second orgasm it took in getting it there.

My brother was born in a hospital an hour south of our home in Jackson Hole. It was the same day I got home from school and found my dog, Gretchen, dead underneath the kitchen table—poisoned by neighborhood boys. Eight years later, Aaron became paralyzed after a trip to Disney World—heatstroke after too many bounces on a trampoline. Mom, the good Catholic dutiful wife, said it was not our affair after she found me in a closet screaming at God, "You son of a bitch!" I was wailing into a tea towel pilfered from the kitchen. She said to be thankful and to pray and that we had to surrender to God's will and count our blessings. Count. Sometimes bad things happened to good people, including the fact that Aaron now sounded like Stephen Hawking as he had to speak through a keyboard. She would say this and rub the top of my head and then put the back of her hand on my cheek and slide it down to my chin. Dad was too drunk to care about my great young crossroads in life.

Surrender to God? And get lost in the count? Screw that.

God out. Blair Wingfield in.

I figured out early on that I was an agnostic, a nonbeliever. In my past life, I was an agnostic, too. I'm a paradoxical moron.

I became a deputy sheriff for Teton County at a fairly young age. Might as well take life into my own hands if God was *in absentia*. Latin was my better subject in high school, but I failed my final exam my senior year because I was making out with a woman ten years my senior behind the outbuildings of the rodeo stables. Her hair was yellow and gold and her husband would have surely shot me. Her tongue felt swollen and hard, her lips small and silky soft. My knees buckled and I was glad to be conjugating her mouth and not Latin verbs. When she pushed her thigh into my crotch, I felt my first involuntary response of throb and release, peak and valley. The wet ran down my legs and into my dirty socks.

I graduated anyway. Cogito ergo sum—*I think therefore I am*. Cunnilingus et puellae—*women and "swabbing the deck."* My first glimpse at another dimension—some people call it heaven. Others call it the little man in the boat. If you ask me, I don't want a man in my boat, little or not.

I liked uniforms and guns and cars with blue lights and sirens. Deputy dyke Fife it was for one Blair Wingfield. At twenty, I passed my entrance exams and graduated second in my class at the police academy behind Oneida Darden, my Hispanic African American sidekick. We were like the Lone Ranger and Tonto but without the mask and Indian outfit.

For the next fourteen years, I watched my mother and father divorce, our country go to war in Iraq and Afghanistan, and our first African American President get into office during the worst economic meltdown since the Great Depression. My best friend Margie, who had taught me how to drink and smoke cigarettes, moved to California to find tattoos, men and her dream of making money. I tried sex once with a man and felt like I would puke. Then, I got in and out of two relationships with women, one straight and experimenting, one alcoholic. Soon after, I became the sole proprietor of my life and my brother's, too.

At thirty-four, two things changed.

Emma Jacobs reappeared in my life after a long hiatus, and the small town of Jackson Hole got its first taste of God truly turning His head in the spring of 2011.

Saturdays meant going to Aaron's favorite place, Flapper Jack's, and then to the Jackson Drugstore for homemade ice cream. I donned my old Amelia Earhart bomber hat and rode my bike into the town square while Aaron motored his wheelchair with the rainbow flag on it behind him. His gallant show of support for me. For the most part, I'd stopped hiding my sexuality the Christmas after high school when I got into a fight with my mother after coming out to her and my dad. It was a grand drunken holiday dinner and I ruined it with the old, "I'm gay, pass me the mashed potatoes" routine. Mom cried for six months and Dad told me it was a phase. She told me to my face that she'd rather have me in a wheelchair like Aaron and stricken with some sort of spina bifida than have the plague of homosexuality. So, in reverence for their support of me, I cut my hair shorter, held hands with my straight girlfriend and went to gay anything: festivals, meetings, organizations and bars. But, you had to go to Denver to find a gay bar. Not a single one in the entire state of Wyoming. That's, of course, because there were no gay people in it. We were just pretend gay people.

Jackson Hole was a hole. A depression of land and log cabins and lights lying flat in the middle of three gargantuan mind-blowing purple mountain majesties behind the skyline of the Grand Tetons. The pompous old western canteen of a town nestled in a quaint stretch of valley known as the gateway town to Yellowstone National Park, a national treasure and part and parcel of the old and new frontiers. A billion tourists a year came to ski, hike, climb, fish, goggle the views and tube the Snake River. But, who was counting?

The town square in Jackson Hole is just that—a square. But, on each corner are the famous hallmark elk horn arches. You can sit on the cement foundations of anyone of them at any corner of the day and see the Gros Ventres Mountains on the east and the Wyoming Range on the south that created the hole Jackson has found itself in. Just around the bend on Highway 22 you could drive five miles west and become catatonic from the majesty of the brilliant Teton Mountains that jut up toward the sky at altitudes of thirteen thousand feet or more. The mountains cut into the air in large jagged peaks that have open air spaces cut out in between like missing pieces in a jigsaw puzzle.

The mystery of the Tetons goes back millions of years ago. When the tectonic plates beneath the ocean clashed like the Titans and the ground and rock swelled up through the water and dirt to breathe its first breath, to unveil its mystery to the world, nature must have bent down in dumbfounded reverence.

Native Americans were the first to see the awesome gallantry of the mountains. Today, visitors from all over the planet visit here to get their fill of horses, stagecoaches, rodeos and the grandeur of the lesser mountains Jackson owes to the grandeur of the Tetons that poets came to write about and artists came to paint. Everyone is a sucker for the Grand Teton, the one in the middle that's the peak, which from the right view is cocked a little to the left as if it were looking down at the fauna and flora and people and asking the same mystical question: who are you littlings? You tiny creatures that like ants crawl on me and study my face, my shadow, my image?

I cackled at my dumb thought and yelled at the Hawk to hurry up. "Can't you pop a wheelie, Aaron, and get your mobile home to move faster?"

My brother was too busy moving his wheelchair to type his Stephen Hawking answer into his keyboard but I saw his head roll back in laughter. Once we got to the northeast corner of town square, Aaron stopped and began waving to a woman on the street like he had cerebral palsy. I stopped my bike and got off and began hooking it over as I heard a voice call, "Hello, Aaron."

When I looked up, I squinted because the sun was momentarily in my eyes. Then they landed on Emma Jacobs, daughter to the Mystic Market's Antichrist, Fannie Crabwell. The town's one and only psychotic Tarot reader you either loved or hated. I hadn't seen Emma in five or six years, not since she'd finished school and gone off to Yale to teach us all a lesson that we should study words and Pythagorean theorems. Her IQ was off the charts. I think she finished high school at twelve and law school by twenty, but I was bad at numbers.

"Hey, handsome, Aaron. How are you?" She walked across the street from the Jackson Drugstore. She held a large bag of groceries and was wearing a green North Face jacket, light enough for the sunny March air.

"Emma, smarty pants, Jacobs! How are you?" I yelled at her but she kept her eyes fixed on Aaron.

She knelt down next to Aaron and I swear he swooned. He typed into his keyboard, then hit the enter key. "I'm. Fine. How's. Your. Cat?" The Hawk's words dulled out into the air like metallic iambic pentameter.

"Oh!" She stood up and continued to ignore me. "He's fine. Just a bad limp. Dr. Evans put him on some medicine to help his joints. I read your first draft, Aaron. I really enjoyed it."

"Hey, Emma..." I said weakly, taking a step forward and removing my flappy bomber hat.

It took her a second to look at me, then I figured it out. She was mad, irritated.

"Blair," tersely.

For only a split second she glanced my way and then looked

back at Aaron who I thought would have an apoplectic fit while conversing with her. I could see why. Emma was classically beautiful. Her long sandy blond hair was parted in the middle and did a sweet cascade down the symmetrical sides of her face. Her light crystal silver-blue eyes were huge. I could barely stop looking at them. Emma had grown up gorgeous. And she wore no makeup and needed none. The porcelain skin glowed like an aura or a light or a candle...I could not think. It was part of the magic that was making Aaron faint all over himself.

At five foot eleven and a hundred and sixty pounds, I towered over her five and a half foot slender frame. I stepped a bit closer and she looked up at me. "Blair," she shifted her groceries, "I see you and Aaron here are out for a Saturday walk in the park." Her lips were pursed downward and tight and she kept shifting her eyes to Aaron who began typing again on his keyboard.

"We've only got wheels, Aaron has four. I've got two. Welcome back to Jackson. Haven't seen you in a while. I guess Yale was good, eh?"

"Yes, I found out a lot about life at Yale. But I'm glad to be back with Mom. I'm working at the old Allen Law Firm, and teaching writing at the rec center. You still at the sheriff's office? I haven't seen you in court." Her clipped pithiness was funny and sexy all at the same time.

"Emma, I'm flabber-busted. I didn't know you were an attorney. Wow, at what, twenty-five? What's next—NASA and the moon? And, yes, I'm still at the sheriff's office on patrol mostly but have been working the jail for a bit. I'm surprised our paths haven't crossed before now. Sometimes small towns are big enough, I guess."

Aaron hit enter. "Where's. Your. Boyfriend. Emma? Have. You. Broken. Up. With. Him. Yet. For. Me?"

"Evan's over in Wilson mucking stalls for one of his buddies and taking some spring tourists out on the trails. I'm almost twenty-seven." Emma looked at me then didn't say a word.

"Emma, you sure are more vocal these days. How did that happen?" I thought, oh no, not Evan Adams. My best friend Margie's old boyfriend from high school. The town's answer to the Marlboro man.

"Talking more to people I like and less to people I don't. You just happen to be a witness today to someone I like."

What a weird trip. I looked at Aaron who was smiling at me and then at Emma.

"What did I do?" I asked.

The Hawk broke in. "You. Arrived. With. Me. Good. Emma. Is. My. Teacher."

"Blair," she whispered and then took me aside, her arm under my elbow as if we were slightly cordial. "Diana tells me that you and Mom fight all the time. What's the deal?"

"For some reason, she hates me. She's the Antichrist, Emma. When did you not see that one growing up? How did you get to be so normal in such a cataleptic insane household?"

"Same way you got to be gay in yours."

"Ouch. For a woman of few words, you find the stinging ones. Shall I give you an Indian name? One Who Flaps Wild Winging Words?"

"Good. Blair. Good," she said, then readjusted her groceries.

I put my hat back on. "See what I mean. See what I mean? Aaron?" I raised my arms up into the air.

"Your brother is a good writer. I'm glad to have such a good student in my adult class. Aaron, I look forward to more." She smiled at him and he gave his okay sign and I wanted to throw up.

"Get a room, you two." I laughed then walked over to Aaron, moved his keyboard into his side holster and then sat on his lap. An act that seemed to surprise Emma.

Her words came out in both disdain and surprise. "Aren't you going to crush him?"

"Come down to the Mystic, Emma, and I'll buy you a beer. Now that you're back in town, you need to come and see the place more often. Bring your boyfriend."

"He doesn't like the place. Says it's too airy fairy for him and his religion."

"Well, maybe you need to quit dating the Christian loser and come and date Aaron."

I wiped the drool off Aaron's face with his neck towel and he turned his mobile motor home toward Flapper Jack's where we'd spend some money on clothes, music for the bungalow, and play poker in the back with six or seven of the town cronies. Emma walked away with her large sack teetering in her small arms.

Most notable about our first meeting in quite a while was how the spirited energetic shift in her saw the spirited energetic shift in me. At least that's how I perceived it, thinking on it later. Her growing up and becoming a Yale graduate, an attorney, and a creative writing teacher returnee to her roots—me a community college graduate, sheriff's deputy and keeper of the Hawkmeister. Egads. What a dueling dynamic difference. So, alliterative. So dumb. But, I smiled anyway.

Once inside and at the back of Flapper Jack's, I held Aaron's cards and he pointed to the chips and what to do. Emma lingered in my mind for quite a while as I tried to figure her out. Another straight cutie who confused me. As I picked up cards and chips for Aaron through the dinge of smoke, I began to see her more and more in my mind's eye. The memories of Emma were few. I could see her with her Aunt Diana, the owner of the Mystic Market, and her crazy mother Fannie—head psychic in charge. My memory of her while she was growing up was how she didn't say much but was sober and cute and loved to eat Cheerios cereal straight out of the box, pinching them into her mouth one at a time. On occasion, we'd played checkers while she drank chocolate chip milkshakes. Once or twice, I remembered helping her with a hard puzzle Fannie had laid out for her on a card table in the corner of the tiny library inside the market. Fannie would shake her finger at me and say, "She'll beat you every time. She knows how and doesn't miss a trick. That's why God put her right here in front of you."

When we got home from our Saturday outing, Aaron put his hands to his head. A migraine. He got them about once a month and sometimes I waited too long to give him his medicine because it would make him sick to his stomach. Everything, it seemed, made him feel sick.

"It. Feels. Like. My. Head. Is. Going. To. Ignite." Aaron flipped out of his chair and got in bed. I closed the blinds then turned off the mute button on my cell. It whirred that it had a message, but I ignored it while I was trying to help Aaron.

"Here, take this vitamin C powder. It will make you feel strong and virile. I promise." I put the glass to his lips and he drank it. It took twenty minutes to get it all down and then I put a wet cloth around the back of his neck. He smiled a faint smile at me and closed his eyes. He lay in a slight, knee-up repose and I pulled the blanket over him.

"You want a little light music to help your head, or just the quiet?" I asked.

His keyboard was at his side and he used one hand to type. "Birds. I. Just. Want. To. Listen. To. Them."

"Gotcha, bird man from Jackson Hole," I said, then leaned over and kissed his forehead lightly. I slid his favorite music magazines over to the edge of his side table and looked out the window at the side of Cache Creek Canyon.

I stepped gently away and spoke under my breath, "Don't mess with him, God. Do you hear me, God. I'll take you to court over this one…and, you won't win. I promise."

I went into my bedroom and lay on my bed. I stretched out fully clothed and put both arms out to the side of the bed. "I will sue you for messing with my brother, God. If you can hear me. I will. I will sue your sorry satanic ass in front of the whole freakin' universe. The jury will be me, God. You won't win. I can promise you that. You will not win."

While Aaron tried to sleep off his headache, I deliberated some more and got up and decided to go down to the Mystic Market to talk to Diana about my troubles with the Archbishop of Devildom, Fannie. And, how her niece Emma, could be so thoughtful and smart and her mother the exact polar bear opposite.

I changed shirts and looked in on Aaron. I put some covers over his feet and then placed my hand on his side and let my eyes cover his body with a sisterly love. I looked out the window to see a red-tailed hawk resting on the split-rail fence just in back of the bungalow. I noticed its large beak and the regal eyes. Two robins landed in the small yard where old piled snow still melted into the mud and grass. Suddenly, I longed for something deep inside me to come alive and to sense the aliveness of the nature around me. But, when I looked down, I thought, how could I sense the aliveness, the vibration of nature in its own brilliance when my brother lay imprisoned in his own head, his own body?

Feeling sorry for birds, and brothers, and my lonely single self, I went to the market in search of solace, perhaps to figure things out. The whys of mothers and fathers, religion and elusive sex in the two partners I'd had since graduating from Teton High School.

The ancient Mystic Market looked like an old log cabin with several additions attached to it and several rustic outbuildings. It lay on a large stretch of spacious land next to Cache Creek. The wood itself was charmingly old, yellowed and splintery. Built as a fisherman's outpost in Jackson in 1938, it became more of a market in the fifties because of the supply and demand of hunters, skiers and tourists who needed food and a place to rest. It looked like a lodge and the current owner, Diana Tucci, had established the country cove as a place to do just about anything—shop, eat, hang out, get your palm read. Anything. Tourists from all over were attracted to the market for its long history as well as for its excellent food, great wares and magical lore. Cache Creek cornered its backside around a line of pine trees where the last of summer inner tubing took place in the last week of August. My favorite sporting activity—anything in water.

The Mystic Market had everything you needed in a town with a lot of regular bored people in it: regular market stuff like Fritos and Mountain Dew and a small counter that served breakfast, lunch and dinner. Then there was the mystic stuff: runic stones, gems and geodes, Tarot cards, psychic drivel and palm reading, candles that smelled like everything from vanilla to Roman Catholic ass, and books. Books about The Presence, The "I Am" Discourses, Buddha, the Unveiled Mysteries, Taiwanese Sex, Chinese herbal medicine, Irish Catholic diatribes, Taoism, Islam, Mohammed, the Spanish Inquisition, the Irish Potato Famine, chicanery wiccan, real wiccan and just the extemporaneous wiccan. The outside of the A-framed log cabin was drizzled with glowing lights of yellow, purple, blue and white. There were statues of the Virgin Mary, Columbus, Walt Whitman, Curious George, St. Augustine, St. Germain, St. Everyone plus Sacagawea and Sasquatch.

The smell of the market was infused with grease, sweet breads and incense of sandalwood. Whenever I smelled this, it made me go inside to a place hollow, long forgotten, like unknown, yet home. The pathetic poet in me was starting to emerge. I really must be hungry.

Down the middle of the market were three glass tables where gem stones and geodes were displayed, small soapstone trinkets of Buddha, rocks of all types and amulets. On the left side of the market was the lunch and dinner counter as well as two aisles of snack foods, beer, wine and fishing tackle. In the far back behind the velvet curtain, Fannie Crabwell and her sister, Diana, would read cards, palms and sometimes psychic energies. Horseshit. Just like God but in a different guise.

Diana, whose silky gray hair contrasted with her dark velvet dress, was bent over figures and complaining about money when I arrived for a glass of beer and some food. Diana was an old Italian hottie, slender and moody and revered by the townies as an adroit businesswoman with a panache for attracting men, women, and most anyone into believing everything she said. I'd known her since I was a kid. She was a surrogate mother and landlord to me since my mother went off to Florida to find a better state, Anita Bryant, and her second husband. Fannie was Diana's sister and icy nemesis to me.

"Did you hear about your dad today?" Diana took off her reading glasses and leaned back in her chair. Three people entered from behind and the wind nearly blew my Amelia hat off.

I grabbed a beer out of the refrigeration cooler and plopped down next to her on a stool. "No, I've been with Aaron all day. My cell's been off. I can't stand the thing when I'm not working. Why? What's up?"

Diana took the beer away from me and took a swallow then stared through the window momentarily. Her newest pooch, which she affectionately called Anika, was romping by the old outbuilding with another neighborhood dog. At the look on Diana's face, I unzipped my jacket and reached for my phone.

When she spoke, the tone was tight, edgy. "He's okay...but, the rest is not good news. I just spoke with Oneida. She called looking for you. She came by about a half hour ago."

My hair stood on end all the way up the back of my neck. "What is it? What's going on?"

"I figured you must be with Aaron playing poker or out riding around listening to music…" She took another hard swallow. "Blair, your dad found one of the female students at Teton High hanging by a rainbow flag underneath the basketball hoop around lunchtime today. She's dead, Blair. A small ladder was kicked over on the floor."

"What! What! Who was it?" I demanded. "I know it's my day off but something like this? Why wasn't I notified? Shit. Aaron must have turned my radio off. He does that sometimes to listen to his music." I shifted in my seat and leaned closer to Diana. "Who was it?"

"Grandy Martinez's daughter, Mary Louise. Evidently, she was the star of the basketball team. I guess she was a lesbian considering how she tied herself up. And, you know Coach Palonski's policy on lesbians."

My stomach turned sick and green and twisted till I thought I might burble up some vomit. "I thought Coach Palonski was cool with the gay girls by now." I stared through the window at my and Aaron's bungalow.

"Emma told me she once saw on the locker room wall 'no alcohol, no drugs, and no dykes,'" Diana said, then replaced her glasses on her nose.

"Sounds like Coach Palonski went to Penn State. They had the same reputation till the coach finally resigned some years back. Quite the brouhaha. Did Oneida say if her parents have been notified?" I watched two or three locals meander into the bar. One headed to the back to get a psychic reading, the other approached the library to peruse the books.

"Your sheriff pal, Oneida, went over there after your dad called the police and told them. Evidently her body is at the coroner's office because they have to rule it was accidental." Diana grabbed my beer and drained it.

I was stunned. An image of Mary Louise hanging from the basketball hoop flung itself into my brain. A very public display of death by hanging in a public arena. Holy cow. The awfulness of it all crept into the thickness of my chest, right in the middle. I covered it with my hand and felt a press like I'd never felt before. Then my stomach rumbled more green and melancholy.

I'd seen her play ball the year before at the state finals in Casper. Her three-foot jumper from the baseline extended was impeccable.

CHAPTER TWO

My father, David Wingfield, became the head janitor of Teton High School in January of 2011. After Mom left him because of the booze, he went from job to job till he landed the big one cleaning toilets and mopping up after snotty-nosed kids. He worked day shift and weekends as needed. Their divorce was Aaron's and my paradise lost. He couldn't quit vodka and she couldn't quit nattering as she had EPD, external processing disorder. Everything that hit her brain ejected itself through her mouth. My own addition to the DSM-IV while taking Psychology 101.

My longing for justice over everything God couldn't handle came after an associate's degree and my first long affair with a woman from the sheriff's department. After our affair ended over a fight about a word I made up in Scrabble, she later helped me land the job where I could wear a brown uniform, a large Batman belt with a radio, handcuffs, bullets, a nine millimeter pistol and wear a hat. Paradise was regained here as I worked as an assistant to investigation and courtroom security when needed. Patrol was my main gig and my favorite as it got me out of the office and into the wild Wyoming wind. I worked ten-hour days, four days a week, rotating shifts to accommodate other officer schedules, weekends and holidays.

Diana pulled me from my trip down memory lane and patted my leg. "Her parents live over at the poorer south end of town near the rodeo grounds. They all went to the Catholic church with Fannie on most Sundays. Mary Louise and Emma knew each other fairly well, I think. I'm pretty sure Emma taught her writing at the rec center." Diana waved to Tyler, the bartender, to bring us both another round of beer. I blew off the beer knowing I'd be driving shortly.

"Does Emma know?" I asked.

"That I don't know since I've been with hysterical systerical. She's in the back doing readings. It calms her down. She really loves that family and loved that girl. She comes out every now and again and just sits and stares at me, and then when she starts to cry, she goes out back to play with Anika and adjusts the bird feeders. Emma should know, though. It's my thinking that they were pretty close as teacher and student. I can't leave Fannie right now. Maybe you could go over and check on things with Emma and her boyfriend and let her know for me. I don't want to tell her on the phone and I trust you. You've done this before, right?"

I had done it before, a miserable part of the job. "I'll call it in right now. I need to go in to work anyway, I'm sure. This is catastrophic." I got up from the table and put my bomber hat in my jacket pocket. "Thanks, Diana. This is truly terrible news. Where is Emma living?"

"On Hansen Street. Twelve-nineteen. Three blocks down from the old library and where you used to live."

"I'm on my way. Shit."

Suddenly, Fannie came out from the back room and saw me. "Get out of here with that droolery brother of yours, where is he?

Hanging. She was hanging. And my Tarot cards went missing from my special shoebox. That's no coincidence Ms. Agnostic!"

"Fannie, with the event of today, you can officially call me an athe-i-ass."

"Father Mark is going to anoint you into the canon of the angels of darkness." She smacked Diana on the back and stared at her. Diana ignored her.

"You might be a while, Blair," Diana suggested.

"I'll check on Aaron before I head over to Emma's but will you check on him in a while, too? He's sleeping but has one of his infamous headaches." I glanced at Fannie who was sticking her tongue out at me.

I stuck mine back out at her and said, "Bring old Fannie with you to check on Aaron. You can read him his cards, Fannie."

Just then, my father walked into the Mystic. The sun was setting and I got up and went over to him.

"You've heard?" His eyes were tired and his speech slurred. He was still wearing his janitorial uniform and he smelled like Clorox and whiskey.

"Yes. You okay?"

"Your boss questioned me for a few hours. I saw Mary Louise's parents come in. It's bad, Blair. The father was only speaking Spanish. The mother tried to translate through her sobbing. It's really bad. I just left and the principal is there along with some of the players from the team and the coach."

"Ten-four. I'm out of here to run a few errands."

Leaving the Mystic Market, I ran to my bungalow. I threw my brown, wrinkled sheriff's uniform on my bed, which was covered in a flannel American flag quilt my mother had bought me. The room was decorated by me: a simple flannel dyke reality show in the making. A brown rickety side table with a sorry lamp, a three-quarter bed on cinder blocks and a large antique dresser Mom gave me in an attempt to make me straight, I think. It had a large mirror and ornate lined scribbling that meandered all over itself as if it were sick of it too. My head started tinkering, wandering. The inmates at the jail were tiresome, gooey, stinky and lonely. Like me in the ruts of my days, the ruts of my nights.

It came to me as I went into the bathroom to brush my

teeth and gaze into the smoky mirror that, yes, I was lonely too. Lonely with the humdrum days of tasking with the inmates and then coming home to Aaron and his ongoing physical maladies. I loved him but grew tired sometimes of his neediness, of someone who was handicapped. Of course, I would never say this to him but my guess was that he knew his suffering added to mine in the way that siblings do to one another. Poor Blair Ignatius Underwear. *Get over yourself.*

I combed my long, straight auburn hair to match my long, straight freckled body. My green eyes were too close together and my nose too large for my sunken, drawn ashy face. I spat the toothpaste into the sink and turned on the water. At thirty-four, I looked more like forty-four. The wrinkles around my eyes were cavernous and the two wrinkles between my eyes were ruts themselves from too much worry over my brother, the state of the ingrates inhabiting the Mystic Market, and the usual ingrates inhabiting the planet. Irritants to send anyone through the ether early to find a better home. *Ahhh, future lives?*

Out of the bathroom, I grabbed my Leatherman and my wallet and clipped my phone to my pants.

"Do. You. Want. To. Read. My. Manuscript?" Aaron considered my countenance. I crossed my eyes at him.

"You must be feeling better, eh? How long have you been working on that book of yours, Aaron?"

"It's. Not. A. Book. It's. A. Manuscript." He hit enter and then motored his wheelchair past the small dining room table to his area of the bungalow. He had a large desk with a computer next to a motorized bed and portable handicapped pot right next to it that my Dad had rigged up. His computer screen was huge and he had pictures of his favorite musicians, mostly women, all over his desk. Heart—Nancy playing guitar. One of his favorite songs was "Barracuda." His iPod had Bose speakers attached to it that he bought with his disability check. Sarah Mclachlan—*Fumbling Towards Ecstasy*. He'd gotten that picture signed when we went to a concert in Cheyenne four years earlier.

A picture of Melissa Ferrick and Melissa Etheridge. He put them there for me. He also had his male musicians: Led Zeppelin—a picture of Jimmy Page with a manufactured autograph. The Rolling Stones, Van Morrison, Elton John, Nirvana, Phish, and Barry Manilow, Air Supply and ABBA. Aaron was cool and sappy and everyone in Jackson Hole loved him.

Diana Tucci was also my landlord as the Mystic Market had made enough money through the years to build small rentable log cabin bungalows. Stephen Hawking lived with me because he couldn't stand Dad's drinking. Dad couldn't care for him anyway. He simply didn't care and had said so on one drunken occasion. Good boy. Mom was long gone with a new husband to Florida. She wrote to me three times a year: Christmas, Easter and my birthday. Her notes always said the same thing. *I love you. Please visit. Tell Aaron to wear more hats when he goes outside.* I write back an echo: *I love you. I will visit. Aaron needs more hats. Please send some.*

On his birthday and Christmas, Aaron gets hats from Mom saying crap like, "Disney World," or "The Sunshine State." He chooses the Sunshine State and says through his keyboard:

"Mom. Is. Sending. Me. Covert. Messages. Through. The. Hats. Do. You. Read. Them?"

"Yes," I say back in my Stephen Hawking metallicky, computery dialect. "Do. You. Feel. The. Need. To. Send. Her. One. Back. Brochacho?" one of my several terms of endearment.

"No. Thank. You. Perhaps. I. Could. Send. The. One. That. Says. Disney. World. Kind. Of. Hurts. Here," he placed his hand on his head and then to his heart. "Know. What. I. Mean?"

As I spoke to Aaron, I readjusted and pulled on the loose door to our tiny home to keep in the warmth. The kitchen held an old black iron skillet I never used, a teakettle I had bought at Martha Pinkerton's yard sale and a blue rubber rack that held dishes to dry. The sink had a window where there were pictures on the sill of Aaron and me and Oneida at a concert for some rock band I could not remember. A picture of our old dog Gretchen in a black-and-white photo and a picture of Mom and Dad when they were pretending to be happy during Christmas in 1984. Then my favorite, one of Aaron and me tubing Cache Creek on my thirtieth birthday. We had strapped him onto a tube and had tied it to mine. His face was agape with a wild expression of,

"I'm FREE and FREAKY!" That's the note we put underneath the picture.

Placing a half-empty box of Cheerios in the cupboard, I turned on my radio and called Oneida. She told me every detail about the hanging, including a detail which I did not expect.

Oneida sighed heavily. "They found a note, Blair. Frightening evidence. It's some heavy stuff. I can't even begin to tell you on the phone. Get your ass to the office. I was first on the scene. The note was stuffed in her mouth."

My knees got weak and I slipped by the kitchen table. Aaron typed into his keyboard.

"Grace."

"Shut up."

I put my belt on and checked my weapon. My radio went on channel three and I kissed Aaron on the forehead. He was playing Heart on his iPod. I could hear them softly singing.

Aaron hit enter and let the words fly. "Out. To. Find. A. Criminal?"

"Ooooo. Barracuda. Yes! I'll be back. Diana and evil Fannie might be by to check in on you."

"Why. Does. She. Call. Me. The. King. Of. Drool. All. The. Time?"

"Because someone's got to be King around here. You good?"

He gave me his okay signal and put his head back on the pillow, slightly, carefully. Sweetly. Just like the man he was.

Speeding away to Hansen Street brought back a flood of memories. Most of what I remember from growing up was lugging my trombone to Teton Elementary School and lugging the thing back, day in and day out. A scene from the mythic Sisyphus: up the hill, down the hill. I finally gave up on the trombone for the flute. I was trying to get in touch with my feminine side to please my mother.

One day during sixth grade when I realized I wanted a guitar, some suspenders and a red alligator shirt that matched everything, I flung the flute out the band room window.

The house Emma lived in was behind a row of scraggly frail bushes and had a cryptic scary feel to it. The shingles needed painting and the apex of the house looked like it had a turret, something out of a Harry Potter film. I hoped I wasn't about to stumble on three kids, a witch and an old wise man holding a scepter.

I rang the doorbell. I put my thumbs in my Batman belt and peeked around at the side bushes where two chipmunks played schizophrenic mating games around the old oak tree. Tools were strewn about in the yard. Then, I looked up at Snow King Mountain issuing its license to the eastern sky just six blocks down. I must have skied that mountain a billion times in the last twenty or more years.

The door opened with soft creaks and Emma appeared with her hair in a ponytail, and a book in her armpit. A V-neck T-shirt was draped over her modest, curvy frame and her firm legs were tight into a pair of jeans that flared at the bottom. Her creamy skin seemed to find my eyes even before I could find the path to her large blue eyes that emitted starry flecks like she was her own constellation. A black cat gingerly snaked around her legs and then sat at attention holding its front paw up and to the side. The injured one, I presumed.

"Hey, Emma," I said. I felt stiff and confused by what I saw.

"Hey, Blair, what's up? Twice in one day?" she asked and then reached down and picked up the cat.

"Nice kitty," I said then reached out to pet it.

Emma dropped the book on the threshold and put her arm out to stop me. "Don't touch him. He'll bite. Gabriel's a biter."

I quickly withdrew my hand and got down to business. "Emma, have you heard the news about Mary Louise Martinez? You may not have. I'm sorry to be here to tell you—"

"She's one of my former students from my night class at

the rec center. I've seen her play ball a few times. Is everything okay?" She nudged the door wider.

"Emma, I hate to tell you this but she's dead. They found her body this morning hanging at the Teton High School gym. She killed herself."

"Oh, Jesus, Mary and Saint Joseph!" She grabbed her chest and dropped the cat to the threshold. "Come in, Blair. Come in. I'm stupefied. Oh, God...unbelievable!" She put her hands to her head.

I walked into her home and found it to be opposite of what the outside intimated. There were pictures of her and Fannie all over the entranceway walls and candles were lit at tiny shrines in the corner near the kitchen and to the left near the living room. As we walked into the living area, votive candles were darting flames, and I saw legal books strewn on the coffee table and a stack of bills neatly laid on an end table. The TV was muted but on CNN. A cup of tea was steaming on the table. On the deck just past the living area were French doors, and outside I could see birds hovering over a half-full bird feeder. Chirps and sveers and whistles danced in the air.

When Emma turned to me, she was crying and wiping the tears with the back of her hands.

"Emma, I'm sorry. I'm really sorry to have to tell you this."

"Sit," she commanded through sniffles. The cat jumped on the coffee table and she hustled him off. "Can I get you some tea or coffee?"

I hesitated. I needed to go see Oneida but felt the urgency of the heaviness of the terrible thing, the terrible death, the terrible crisis in a world where we agnostics were bent up in suspended disbelief at the cruelty of life. Finally, I said, "Of course. That would be wonderful."

"Let me guess. Cream and sugar?"

"Yes. Lots of both," I said with a slight bit of embarrassment.

I watched the birds as I shifted nervously on the couch. My eyes turned to CNN where the latest Alaskan oil crisis, as gigantic as the Gulf's the year before, unfurled. When they showed a pelican gasping for its life, struggling through the thick and goo, I wanted to grab the clicker and change the channel. Animal struggles were a soft spot for me. I could see dead bodies and maiming all day long, but an animal trapped or hurt or abused made me sick to my stomach. I put my thoughts to the lit candles and the tiny Jesus shrines.

"Why all the candles?" I asked as Emma came back into the room with the steaming cup of java.

She handed it to me and sat in her recliner. "For Mom. She comes by all the time. She loves candles and I have to remind her all the time when she's in her own house to blow them out before she goes to bed or she'll burn everything up." She grabbed her tea and we were silent.

I sipped my coffee and stayed with the space the silence created, not forcing or doing anything till Emma was ready. Gabriel the angelic biting cat jumped on the TV and regarded us both with careless cat-like irreverence.

"I'm absolutely dumbfounded. I can't believe it. I just can't believe it," Emma said. "Mary Louise Martinez was the star of my creative writing class last fall. She took it to help her with her SATs because I do a spot on the writing part of that for my younger students. I remember a poem she wrote about an old abandoned school bus and one about the bones of a butterfly. Amazing words. She was talented beyond her age. She—"

"They found a note," I interjected, " but I don't know anything about it. I have to go down to the office and meet Oneida. She was first on the scene. I had my radio off today accidentally or I might have been there."

Emma looked at me, her eyes reddening, throwing her constellation into a different orbit. The weight in my breastbone tightened to see her this way but I held the space to see what she would say next. Then after another sip she said, "I'm going to talk to my buddies at the firm and see what they say about this."

"Your firm?" I almost knocked my coffee over as I set it down.

"The Allen Law Firm," she said and looked at me as quizzically as I was looking at her. "Remember from earlier? I've been working with the Allens since last December. I've argued several small cases but you haven't been in court to witness them."

Just then, a car pulled up.

"That's probably Evan. He's back from Pinedale working with some horses."

"Emma, if you are doing the lawyer gig, then why do you teach at the rec center?" I asked.

She wiped away a few tears. "I like teaching disadvantaged youth and people with disabilities," she said as the door opened. A large, handsome man filled the doorway. He took off his shoes and hat.

No words. Emma rolled her eyes at me and got up.

I eyed Emma and felt immediate tension fill the air between the two of them. Instinctual.

"Hey, Evan…how were the horses? You know Blair Wingfield?" Emma said.

I got up and pulled my brown slacks down to the top of my black leather shoes. Evan came lumbering in smelling like hay and horseshit.

"Hey, Blair Underwear from high school. Yeah, she gave my brother his first and second DUI last year just over Teton Pass when he was coming back from Idaho Falls." He sat down on the chair Emma had been sitting on and grabbed the clicker to change the channel. "Emma, will you get me a beer? Did you all hear about the Martinez girl hanging herself at the school gym today? Jesus Christ. Right on the basketball hoop and a suicide note sticking out of her mouth. What the fuck was that all about?"

"Christ, Evan. She was one of my students!" Emma walked into the kitchen and I followed her.

I wanted to wrap my arms around her as she muttered indecipherably, grabbing a beer and trying to grab some sense.

"Emma. I'm sorry. How he knows, I have no idea…I guess news travels fast in a small town."

"I've been going to church at Lady of the Mount for many years, Blair. The Martinezes go there too. Evan works with the father shoeing horses and training. It's how I met Evan—at church."

"Emma, what are you going to do now?"

"Make a pie, I guess. Make a pie." She paused realizing she'd said it twice. "Then take it over to their house and light a candle. Light a candle. Maybe I'll do that now."

She was trying to hold it together. "Here's my card." I pulled one out of my wallet. "If you need something...anything. Just call or come over. Aaron and I live a drab life but we're safe and easy."

"Hey, where's that beer?" Evan yelled from around the corner.

"Blair?"

"Yes?"

"Mary Louise Martinez was gay."

"Yes."

"You know about the coach's policy on that?"

"Yes. I believe we all saw it through the years."

"What do we do now?"

"I don't know. I'm going to the office to meet Oneida."

"Once this settles down, I'm going to approach her family about taking the case."

I was surprised. "What case Emma? What are you talking about?"

"Blair. You saw the writing on the wall...Blair. The writing on the wall. You saw it. Didn't you play basketball?"

"I was downhill skiing. Too much long hair, ponytails and goggles to notice a lesbian nation."

"But you know what I mean?" Emma uncapped a beer and made a delivery as I walked toward the front door. Gabriel slunk toward both of us.

She put her hands on her hips. "Two times in one day I've seen you now. This is horrible about Mary Louise. Despicable. An innocent young girl lost to a hatred that Wyoming can't seem to shake."

"I know," I said as I put my hat on. "First Matthew Shepard, then *Brokeback Mountain*...then..."

"Blair...this is different."

"How?"

"Matthew was murdered by hatred. *Brokeback* was a movie.

This is not a murder. Not a movie. This is suicide. Hanging. Hanging from a basketball hoop."

"Emma, I hate to say this but you're acting a little trippy here. Plus, we still need to have it ruled a suicide. I just wanted to come by and let you know what happened. I felt the need to do so."

Emma smiled. "If you want trippy, look at my mom. If you want a closer lens on politics, religion and martyrdom—ask me."

I smiled back. "What makes you the expert?"

"Yale."

"Just Yale." I looked toward the cowboy of a boyfriend watching a baseball game on TV. "I guess he was the martyrdom part. What's the sacrifice there?" I whispered, gesturing toward him.

She pulled back as if I'd stung her slightly then said, "My mom likes him and so does Diana and so does—"

"You are corroborating the martyrdom piece here, Attorney Crabwell, I mean Jacobs. Jacobs, right?" I asked.

"It's Jacobs, not Crabwell. I kept my stepfather's name in the divorce. Mom always kept her maiden name."

"Oh, Emma Jacobs. That's not as crabby. Well, Attorney Jacobs. Congratulations on your knowledge of the universe. I'll see you soon. In the meantime, you can still come down to the Mystic even if your boyfriend can't. It's not like we're a gay bar or something."

"Thanks, Blair. You are kind. I will see the Martinezes soon. I hope to see you soon, too."

On the steps, I turned around feeling high and mighty and then I slipped on the first step, evidently some scuffed horseshit and nearly fell off the porch. Emma grabbed me from behind and kept me from going all the way down. We both laughed and I picked up my hat and walked backward away from her waving.

"Tell Evan you'll need a cup of tea soon!"

"Tell my mother to blow out her candles down at the Mystic. I'll see you soon. Thanks for the card. Say a prayer for the Martinez family, Blair. They're going to need it." She closed the door.

Pray? I looked down at my hands and thought about the concept of prayer. I could not wrap my brain around it. It was too out there, too aloof, too churchy, too not me.

Pray rhymed with gay. That's all that came.

And that was what I had to say in Emma's defense.

CHAPTER THREE

Oneida met me in the sheriff's office on North Broadway, three streets over from the town square. As we'd known each other for all the years I'd been doing my Barney Fife routine, her sassiness outweighed her professionalism. Oneida went to the same church as the Martinez family: Our Lady of the Mount. To me it sounded pornographic like a young filly mounting a virgin colt, but I never told Oneida that. She was a tepidly devout Roman Catholic and ate her holy wafer on Sunday with her three small kids: Elena, Peter and Nikki. Each about two years apart from one another. Oneida's husband had left her for another woman almost a year ago and she hated penises more than I did, or at least what they represented: the political phallic forum that most politicians took...the power of the penis no matter how small or big the issue. The Pope was excluded from her phallic nomenclature because, according to her, he only masturbated in his dreams and that was passable.

"Hey, Blair. Geez girl. Where you been?" Oneida said as she ate a protein bar and drank a Slim-Fast. Oneida was about twenty pounds overweight and always on a diet.

I put my keys down on my desk. It was across the aisle from hers in the sheriff's office headquarters adjacent to the courthouse. "I was over at Emma Jacobs's to tell her about the Martinez girl."

"How'd she take it?" She swallowed a bite and then put her feet up on her desk.

"Bad. Upset, I guess. But I think her boyfriend's an asshole. Ever meet him? Evan Adams. He actually works with Mary Louise's father as a farrier."

"Yeah. I met him when he was in court with his brother. The one you caught drunk driving. He's on my list of pathological pinheads."

"What's the scoop on Mary Louise Martinez?" I asked, sitting at my desk. "Have all of her relatives been notified?"

"The coroner will probably rule a suicide, time of death, the usual. The parents are freaked out and upset and went home about an hour ago. Judd should be here any minute to tell us the next step. We're going to have to interview the coach and the team—they were in the gym this morning for an off-season workout. Evidently, everyone left and Mary Louise did what she did. Your dad might be questioned again. We have to treat it as a crime scene till we get the time of everyone's departure from the gym and the time the doors were locked then reopened by your father to clean. Why doesn't he clean on Friday nights?" she asked me.

"Oneida, he has always worked Saturday afternoon because of his very important drinking schedule. He's always at the town dance on Fridays and then he goes over to the Cowboy Bar to shoot darts and drink till they close." I shifted in my seat and fiddled with the radio on my shoulder.

Judd Williams, the town's sheriff, walked in the front double doors and approached us. His uniform was wrinkled and his boots heavy. As he removed his hat, I could see the smeared sweat on his brow, his half-bald head. His beard needed a shave and his belly protruded from over his belt line.

"Here comes the boss," Oneida said and took a swig of her Slim-Fast.

He stopped at our cross-like intersection and looked at me. "Where were you earlier? We called you on your cell and then on your radio."

"Sorry. Aaron sometimes turns my radio off when he's listening to his music or trying to sleep. I wasn't paying attention."

"Well, I guess we have your attention now. This is bad, Blair. Very bad. The local media outlets are already buzzing. If it gets out big, then we may have a goddamn national media scene here. Mary Louise Martinez has a lot to say in that note of hers and if the contents of it leak out now, we're screwed or at least the Teton County School District is."

Oneida threw the wrapper in her trashcan and looked at me and raised both eyebrows. She wanted me to talk.

I stood up and got a notebook and pen and looked at her then at him and exhaled. "What did the note say that's so bad?" I asked.

There was a small pause as Judd shifted his cowboy boots around on the wood floor. "I can't believe she hanged herself in the gym." He had pointedly ignored my question. Odd. "Oneida, have you heard anything from the medical examiner?"

"Not yet. But last I heard, he'll have something for us by morning."

"We need to hold vigil of some sort. Perhaps at the church where she went? Do you think they will let us set up a small command post there for the students and the families and if the media wants to talk we can talk there? I think that might be a good idea." Judd walked back and forth, uneasy. He was making me think that this was too big of a mess for a small town like Jackson to handle. What was in the note?

"You two go on patrol together tonight and be ready for people to be extra drunk and extra unhappy and looking for answers. This girl was a model student, a gifted basketball player, and, I guess, a lesbian. Rainbow flags are lesbian, right Blair?"

"They are lesbian, gay, bisexual and transgender. LGBT," I said and moved uncomfortably in my seat. I knew he knew. It just had never come up before. I was small and inconsequential but this I had to give up to him. The provincial sheriff.

"Okay. I think a command post at the church is a better idea than here for PR purposes. A church is more forgiving than a sheriff's department. Perhaps the media will go easy on us and the school there."

Oneida stood up and stretched her arms. "Sheriff Williams, can you tell us what was in the note so we can be a little prepared? Why are you defending the school system so suddenly, anyway? No one's on trial yet. Hell, we don't even have the coroner's results."

"She has named people on the team who, I guess, bullied her and then she's named the school's resource officer as the person she told at least three or four times. Evidently, and I never knew this, the coach over there has had something to do with it too. Coach Palonski. She's married to Jack Palonski. He's my fishing buddy. I'm just trying to mitigate a bit."

The plot was thickening and the hair on the back of my neck stood up. I'd slept with the school's female police officer three years ago. Her name was Susie Clarkson and she was the biggest Republican dyke on the Jackson police force. Holy dot connection. She voted for Bush both times and was in love with Sarah Palin. We had sex three times on her couch before I became completely grossed out by the inordinate amount of clitty litter she had.

Suddenly, I longed to be at my bungalow checking on Aaron and listening to some music on my iPod while doing a crossword that had Martinez as one of the clues. Who was this girl? Why did she do what she did in such a grandiose way? Talk about sending a message. Media? The only interesting press we ever got was when we helped the Jackson police solve a murder mystery in Yellowstone when some campers went missing.

"Blair, can I count on you to go to the church and help with keeping order? If there is a police officer that is going to get in trouble, then we have to step up our presence. I'll put you in command there with Oneida after I talk to Father Mark. Okay?"

"You got it," I said. "We'll head over there after you notify us that Father Mark is cool and we can set up some lines, cones and a marker of some sort for Mary Louise. We'll go by her parents' house after you tell us."

Raising my eyebrows at Oneida, she raised hers back, then looked at the clock. I followed her eyes to the clock, 7:44 p.m. Saturday night. Last night at this time, Friday, Mary Louise was alive. I wondered if it was then that she had made her plan. An image of her writing a suicide note suddenly popped into my head. I saw her long dark hair in a ponytail. Her room strewn with posters of her favorite rock stars. Jeans and shorts on the bed and her computer stickered with JWY or with pictures of the WNBA, perhaps the Seattle Storm. Who knows.

I got up and walked to the water fountain and took a swallow and then placed my left hand into the stream to grab some liquid. Putting my head down to the fountain, I took the water and rubbed it on my neck, face and head. I stretched my arms to the sky and thought of the Mystic Market and pie. Apple pie. Some forbidden fruit, I mused.

"This is insane. I can't believe it," Oneida said. "We'll patrol till midnight then let Todd and Marty take over till daybreak. They're the new kids on the block but can handle things with the Jackson police till we get back on in the a.m. I have to find a sitter for my kids. You think Emma could sit for them?"

I was roused from my staring at the clock, Mary Louise's image of her room, and a picture of a limping black cat. "Emma? Yeah. Probably...why?"

"Because my sitter can't do it and I'm out of options right now. My brother is out of town; otherwise, I'd ask him. She's seen them at church and in Sunday school." Oneida got up and got her hat.

"I'll call her and see. I don't think it will be a problem. She loves kids from what I can remember, that smarty-pants. Did you know she has been working at the Allen firm since late last year?"

Judd stepped in momentarily. "I've seen her in court. She's quiet but good. A bit standoffish, though."

An image of Emma in court suddenly flashed in my brain. Skirt. White blouse, opened up slightly at the neckline. Small, firm pumps. Hair up and glasses tossed onto a legal pad.

Abruptly, the flashing squeezing sensation entered my lower extremities. No warning. No nothing. Just a hard squeeze from inside that flowed warmly down my legs, like a volcano oozing lava at glacial speeds.

Then my phone rang. Margie Freaking Hostetler.

"Hey, you big deputy dyke loser," Margie giggled at the other end of the phone. "I still hate you but will be there to see you in about two months, anyway. It's been too long and I'll smoke pot out of your handcuffing range."

Walking toward the front of the office, I said, "Marge, you pussy! It's good to hear your gravelly voice. You got cancer yet?"

"No, but I'm bringing my buddy Mick. She's my newest groupie and is the agent to every seventies rock band worth hearing. She's a freakin' Lynyrd Skynyrd slash Eric Clapton whoremonger. Okay if we come and see that stroked out brother of yours? You gotten him laid yet?"

"Yes, please come. Things have gotten pretty weird here." I said this and suddenly remembered how I'd had a secret crush on Margie in school. We ran all over town day and night smoking pot, drinking beer and running in the wild Wyoming wind. On Snow King Mountain, we'd gotten to the top twice and I thought for sure she was my soul mate. But, in her words, she "loved the dick."

Momentarily, I had a fond memory of Margie and me behind the back of the Jackson recreation lodge where my mom and her mom played bridge every Sunday. For four hours, we would run around the rec center while Aaron would play wheelchair basketball in the gym. Evil Margie and me would sneak smokes by the water fountain out back. She had eight thousand freckles on her face and two large blackheads at the top of her nose I was constantly staring at. I found myself secretly squeezing them when she was asleep. Blackheads and zits fascinated me. All that goo coming out of such a tiny hole.

Jackson Hole was a hole. Margie and I survived growing up in psychosis land by drinking, smoking pot and laughing at our inconsequential lives. Townies saw it as a town, no more no less. But high school teenagers like me and Margie saw it as a trap like all high schoolers do. Our long-ago longing to flee was fierce, especially from the nudge of all nudges: parents. Margie showed up for me when Aaron became an invalid and my Mom and Dad became invalids in their provincial lives. Her mom was the town whore and her Dad was a traveling salesman—never around till birthdays, Christmas, graduation and eventual divorce.

Her visit would be good for the humor. Like something out of a John Steinbeck novel, we laid out our best plans for her to come and relieve the stress. A few summer concerts and we could get her and Mick a bungalow two doors down. My good friend…coming to see me and give me a lift.

But, as I've seen in novels and in movies, sometimes the best laid plans of mice and men often go astray.

CHAPTER FOUR

On Sunday, the coroner ruled a suicide. Dad had been smart to leave her as he found her and not mess with the body. Instead he'd run outside and yelled for help and called 911. By the time Oneida got there, Dad was with an old neighbor from across the street who was in his underwear and boots. He'd advised Dad to settle till Oneida got there. Oneida checked Mary Louise's pulse, then roped off the scene and waited for the coroner. Later, she told me she puked in the bushes near the double doors and cried in her squad car.

It was corroborated by the coach that the team had left at eleven a.m. Dad came on at one p.m., giving Mary Louise enough time to off herself. Time of death was placed around noon. It was all nice and tidy. Still, people had to be identified. The locker room searched. The coach and players separated and talked to individually—including Susie Clarkson who would have to be put on administrative leave as the school's police officer—with pay, of course, till things settled down.

Father Mark had given the sheriff's department permission to use the church as a command post for the media to deter anyone from hanging around the sheriff's department, the police department and the courthouse. Like he said, he hoped it would be a mitigating and detracting scene.

I dressed slowly and methodically in my uniform on this particular Sunday, with a more melancholy sense of who I was. The image of Mary Louise hanging under the basketball net with a rainbow flag tied around her neck did double flashes in my mind. I was very interested in the contents of the suicide note and what the students and faculty and resource officer would tell: The truth? Or would they fudge it?

I fiddled with my gun as I thought briefly about life and death. I could easily turn this gun on myself and shoot myself in the head and be done with my own constant questioning. Why Aaron was the way he was. Why the health care system in America was drunk off its money-whoring. Why Emma was straight. Why Fannie was as crazy as bat shit. Why my mother was so far away. Why my father drank himself to blankness. Why my heart was a Carson McCullers reprise. Why people of the planet fought to survive only to be faced with imminent death. Why the worry of money, power, politics, religion. Why the worry of sexuality of any particular type. Why Wyoming for me. Why bad guys and good guys and war and peace. Why the embrace of day. Why the embrace of night. Why Mary Louise Martinez. *Shut up.* I put my hands to my head.

I stopped.

I sat at the edge of my bed.

It creaked.

Aaron stirred.

I looked in the mirror and saw my image blur and fade like I was a ghost. I could only hear the ripples of Cache Creek in the background and the music of the birds opening their throats to spring. Everything smelled like black soot. I had read once about Shakespeare talking of the edge of doom in one of his sonnets we studied in twelfth grade. Mary Louise Martinez had walked the iambic edge of doom Friday and Saturday night. Fleetingly, I could see the coroner poking a hole in her liver to test the warmth to determine her time of death. I held my side. Then I could see Oneida checking her wrist for a pulse. My hand suddenly went to my heart. Ta-tum, ta-tum—a drumbeat. Covering my badge and shirt with my hand, I watched as I reemerged into focus. Then, to my surprise, I saw Aaron sitting in my doorway.

He hit his keyboard. "You. Okay?"

Quickly, I shoved my hand over my gun and put it into my holster then stood up and strapped it on. "I'm good. Guess Diana told you the news. How's your head?"

I sat down and tied my shoes as he typed into his keyboard then waited for him to finish. His hair was muffed up in the back and his drool towel had fallen over the side of his motor home. "You're slow this morning. That manuscript of yours must have hurt your fingers typing it, Stephen King Hawking." I pulled his towel up around his head.

"My. Head. Is. Good…It. Is. Terrible. News. So. Young. Diana. Said. She. Was. Smart. And. Pretty."

He eyed me for a moment. We both waited in the black edgy moment it was becoming.

"Only the good die young…Billy Joel knows it all, doesn't he?" I asked rhetorically.

"Can. You. Eat. Before. You. Go?"

I didn't want to stay. I was impatient for the first time in my life to actually get to a church on time: Our Lady of the Mount.

"I'll only go get a quick bagel with you at the Mystic. And, if you get another one of your headaches, I'm taking you to the doctor, or I'll just pop a cap in your ass and give you something else to worry about." I giggled and put on my sheriff's ball cap. "I'm going to ask Mom to buy you a hat that says, 'cap,' how dumb is that?"

"You're. So. Good. To. Me. A. Cap. In. The. Ass. Would. Feel. Much. Better. Than. These. Headaches." He trolled around in his mobile home and zipped into the living room.

Aaron got his iPod and manuscript to work on while I finished making my bed. Five minutes later, at the edge of our small bungalow, the edge of my own personal doom, I climbed onto Aaron's lap and let him motor his deputy dyke sister to the Mystic for bagels and coffee. Some drool came from his mouth and I quickly wiped it with my jacket.

"What are you going to do today?"

He regarded me with his handsome eyes then placed his keyboard in my lap and tapped. "I'm. Going. To. Play. With. My. Game. Boy. And. Listen. To. Ann. And. Nancy. And. Led. Zeppelin."

"Okay, Stephen Hawking. As long as you don't play with yourself."

Like a Christmas tree, his face lit up in amusement.

"Don't. Fart. Into. A. Paper. Bag. Then. Inhale. Through. It. After. You. Hyperventilate." It took five minutes to tap it out, but I waited and waited and waited. His eternity was worth waiting for.

He'd stay with the magazines, books and company of Diana and Fannie till I retrieved him later.

Peering up into the March sky made me feel like what Van Gogh must have felt, all swirly and colorful in his head and his canvas. The sun cast blues and violets and brown blacks over the sensual, grassy, tree-thick mountains. The crevasses and precipices were showered in a lingering spring mystical show of magical essence—maybe? Evanescent, for sure. My only sanity were the songbirds, the sagebrush, the twilight tinged with an Indian indigo. Oddly or not, they were like my long-lost friends, like the only ones I could count on.

I once heard that large, strange beliefs and bad blood and prejudices and hatred took years, decades, centuries sometimes to heal. The collective pain body of planet earth was in a constant state of healing. At the Mystic, Aaron read all about it and told me that Jesus, Buddha, Ghandi, Tolle, the Dalai Lama, the Wizard of Oz, Oprah, Dr. Oz, Dr. Phil, Ann Landers, Erma Bombeck, Judith Orloff, Pete Townsend and Barack Obama all had the audacity of healing and hope. This was, of course, Aaron's list. I told him I agreed with Erma Bombeck but she was dead, so who did I have now. Aaron's curt response when I said it like this was: "All. You. Have. Is. You. Dummy."

I kissed him on the forehead between his eyes and shoved the last bit of my bagel in his mouth. It was smeared with cream cheese and he laughed so hard that I thought I had choked him.

"Write your bestseller, Aaron, then I can quit my job and take you to an island with palm trees, blue water, hot girls and wheelchair access to a grand pavilion where Ann and Nancy will play just for you…and me, of course."

He smiled at this and then gave me his okay sign as cream cheese fell into his lap.

At the same moment, Fannie walked in. "Dear God, can you give the crip a straw or something?"

"Diana?" I yelled. "If you don't get your sister into treatment, I'll have to start treatment on her myself!"

Oddly, Fannie came over to us. "Emma told me about the Hispanic girl. I'm working on a plan to figure it out."

"Fannie," I said then stood up towering over her five-foot frame. "It was suicide. Pure and simple."

She shook her head almost violently when I said this. "It was no suicide." She grinned then picked up some bacon off a plate on the counter and shoved it in her mouth. "It was a sacrifice. You'll see. I'm working on it." Then she slapped me on the back like she half-liked me, an act that surprised both Aaron and me.

Diana came in from the back with wood in her arms for the fireplace. "What did you want, Blair?"

"Nothing. I'm on my way to church. I'll be back later."

"Be careful out there, Blair. From what I can feel, this is going to be strange. Very strange."

"Okay. Well, maybe you and Fannie and Stephen King here can get it all down on paper for me to check out. Right now, I've got to get to work."

"Light a candle for me this morning, Blair," Diana pleaded. "At the altar they've set up. Light a candle for me and everyone here at the market. I'll be off later and come by to light one myself. Can you do that?"

"Diana, you know I'm not a believer."

"That's why I ask you to do it for me. Not for you, hon." Diana placed the wood in the back near the fireplace.

"Okay. I'll light one for you. But it may get people thinking I've changed my ways."

Fannie chimed in. "It's not about you, Blair."

And, for once, Fannie Crabwell was right.

CHAPTER FIVE

At the moment of commitment, the universe conspires to assist
you.

It was a quote by Goethe that Aaron had on his screen saver.
My conspiracy theory at this time was that I felt Diana may
be correct. She was a gifted psychic like her sister and she had
revelations and "knowings" right down to her root chakra about
situations. I for one believed in her and her ancient mystic ass. I
had all my life, especially the time we saved her dog from being
trapped in one of her outbuildings. It was one of the strangest
days I'd ever had, like a T.S. Eliot still point.

Now, the strangeness of the Mary Louise Martinez's suicide
suddenly took on bone-chilling epic proportions. I flashed once
more to her hanging in the gym. Even though I had not been
there, I could see her body. Sweaty T-shirt from practice, her
head leaning forward with the top of her head swaying slightly
under the net of the basketball rim, the tendrils of rope brushing

the top of her head. I felt the ropey flag twisted about her neck, the hyoid bone broken in the minute she'd kicked over the ladder beneath her. Her tennis shoes dangling like a ballerina's in the struggle it took to strangle the life out of herself. My hope was the struggle had been short and that she'd passed out quickly.

I drove past the town square in my sheriff's Jeep and got right behind a tourist for sure. At the South East elk ivory arch, I sped around the black town car and glanced in the window. For a second, I thought it might be a celebrity, but the window was too dim and I was in a hurry to get to church on time. Oneida had talked with Emma and she'd acquiesced in taking care of the kids if Oneida brought them over to her house on Hansen. She was preparing for a case and could manage herself and them. I thought of Evan and how Emma could have sex with that cowboy bastard. My stomach turned green with hate and envy all at once. Then that ungodly picture flashed. I stopped it the second it got started and clenched the steering wheel harder.

I flew down Broadway toward the church and passed some distant relatives of my high school buddy, Margie Hostetler, walking toward town square. They waved at me and I waved back. Marge would be here in about eight weeks. I couldn't wait to see her and Mick and reminisce about old times when we smoked, drank and saved a trapped dog once from the outbuilding at the Mystic.

We were seniors at Teton High School and I was dying most days to kiss Margie and she knew it. Game play between us.

Margie zipped her coat up and exhaled. "You're the best friend a girl could have."

"Don't be such a pussy, Margie. I hate you."

"I hate you too."

Margie then sprayed me with cologne to cover the smoky smell. *Moron.* I'd rather kiss her or Carleen Proust, the president of the class and the head cheerleader, but I couldn't find the voice to shoulder that dumbass commitment to hell and high water.

My senior year was my formative year and Margie's, too. Bill

Clinton was just entering his second term and if there wasn't God, then there was Bill with his stocky wife and his only daughter Chelsea, who, I'm sure was trying to figure how to smoke cigarettes and drink beer with the Secret Service up her a-hole.

Margie's parents lived ten blocks from my house past Broadway and right behind the Million Dollar Cowboy Bar which sidled itself on the street across from town square. Locals called it the Cowboy Bar and it was where my father and mom spent a million dollars a year on drinking and eating, which was great because I could roam all over town anytime night or day and they really wouldn't know where I was. By the time I was a senior, Aaron was old enough to hang in the house by himself with a Game Boy.

"Blair," said Margie, the swanky sexy bohemian, and shoved her hand in her pocket. "Here's another smoke for you, you Amelia Earhart look-alike."

I pulled my bomber fleece aviator cap down over my ears that stuck out too much and grabbed the lighter and the smoke. "Thanks, and shut up, your camel toe isn't helping your wench-like reputation, whore." She pulled her black jeans down and we both giggled and lit up, inhaling hard at the same time, the same smoky ritual. Her fingernails were alternatively black and purple.

Exhaling like we were both rock stars on break from the first half of the concert, I leaned back next to her and peered up at Cache Creek Mountain abutting the edge of the Elk Refuge a half a mile away, not far from Teton High School.

"My dad's going to go to California this summer." Margie inhaled slowly. "He's got a job in Monterey at one of the canneries. Good money he says. Mom's not so happy about it. But then again, I'm pretty sure she's banging Ray White, our infamous town drunk Dumpster diver, so maybe this wench-like reputation is catchy, like chlamydia."

I puffed out again. "A cannery. That sounds cool. Maybe you can go out and visit the place where Steinbeck used to live. Maybe you can live off the fatta the lan'?"

I paused then continued. "Ray White. He hangs out with

old crazy Crabwell. I see them in town square at the north end of antler-ville. You cool with him grazing your mom's unleashed camel toe?"

"The affair? Yeah, I guess but I don't know why Dad can't work here." She said this then kicked an old can laying in the dirt. "I may go with him. Think you can handle this imaginary farce of a town without me?" She winked.

"I might shrivel up and die from desperation. Hey, my Dad is working a second job cleaning up roads for the Forest Service before summer season hits up near Yellowstone and wants me to help him this weekend. You want to come along and we can start a forest fire or something?"

"Sure. I've got plenty of matches. Jesus. Maybe we can get arrested just a few months before we graduate." Margie wiggled both her eyebrows at me. "I don't know. If they see I'm with Amelia Earhart, they just might cut us some slack." She ruffled my hat and we giggled and ambled toward the Mystic Market. I thought I might burn the market down too, if we were on our pyro tirade. Burn down my burgeoning sexuality with it might make matters better. Kill it all.

For a second I remembered Margie and me riding on inner tubes the summer before. We had bobbed and laughed all the way around the creek, a large wide feminine circle encircling the town. *Nature. Emerson was right. Like a lonely call home.* The Mystic Market was my absolute favorite part of the town because it was nestled next to cool trails, simplicity and solitude, and overall I'm-here-in-the-woods Henry David Thoreau kind of way. Just to keep it simple as those transcendentalists loved, apparently. A slight mist tinged the air and the smoke from the market's chimney was seen above the eight pine trees that cast the night shadow on it. You could smell the smoke from it permeating the air all over town.

Then we heard the panicked yell.

We hauled ass.

At the outbuilding behind the store was gyrating gypsy Diana, maker of the colossal myriad of oddities, holding a pickax in one hand and a flashlight in the other. She was yelling for someone to help her. "Jesus Christ, someone help me! It's Lexi!"

Margie said it first. "God! It's the grandma reaper!"

I laughed and then skidded face-first on the dirt road. Margie reached down and offered a hand. She pulled me up then winked at me. My stomach fell and I broke into a run, the flaps of my jacket waving up and down in the wind of the expansion of the run, to fly to get away!

Underneath the outbuilding we thought we heard the dog rustling and Fannie was on her knees in full prayer mode. Her young daughter, Emma, stood beside her looking from person to person and every now and again would slide her hand in a box of Cheerios and eat an O or two. Fannie put her arms out and up as if she were doing the touchdown prayer and I crossed my eyes at Margie. She crossed hers back.

"Blair Underwear, come with me to the side over here." I followed her and patted Emma on the head as Margie and I knelt down in front of the shed and hollered alternatively for Lexi to either whine or come on out.

Diana threw her hat down into the mucky dirt. "Can you all hear anything? She must have been chasing that damn rabbit again. I could hear her whine from inside then I heard nothing. Nothing when I got out here."

Evan, Margie's on-again off-again boyfriend, came bounding from around Starling Road, grabbed her pickax and began hammering on the back of the shed. Splinters and pops, pops and splinters echoed across the creek and into the canyon next to Snow King Mountain. I knocked on the wall and put my head and body facedown in the dirt to see if I could see a whisker or line of dog hair.

Ten minutes later, Fannie showed up with her own dog, old limpy Anika. They were limpy kissing cousins. Black fur covered the German shepherd as one ear stuck up and the other bent over in a flibberty-gibbety kind of way. Her back legs were hunkered down as her breed assumed and her eyes were of two different colors: one blue, one black-brown.

Margie and I dug furiously with our hands to try and create nose room to peer in. Diana grabbed more flashlights from the Mystic Market and Anika sniffed the perimeter, staying closer to Emma than anyone. For twenty minutes there was mass confusion as Diana wailed for the dog, Evan and I alternatively used the pickax and shovel to create a hole in the back of the shed. Fannie and Emma started removing items from the shed because there were tiny cracks and holes all over the bottom that Diana and Fannie figured were viable ways to see Lexi.

Diana called, "Lexi. Come on. Anika is here."

I looked up. Anika was not by the shed. I got up and went back to the doorway. I took a step further, then turned my flashlight back on. Anika was sitting next to Emma getting one Cheerio at a time. The second Cheerio went through a crack near the chest of costumes by a box of books. The third one into Emma's mouth. She pulled one more out and put it in the palm of her hand and jutted it toward me.

When I got to Emma, she handed me the Cheerio and I popped it into my mouth. She grinned at me with her pearly even teeth and she said, "Here." Then she popped another Cheerio into the hole.

I turned the flashlight on and it shined directly into her face. "Sorry, Emma."

"That's okay," she said faintly.

"Drop another one in the hole for me," I said. She did, ever so gently and with precision.

I shined the flashlight into the hole and staring back at me was Lexi, black wet nose and muddied face.

"In here!" I yelled. "She's in here." When the entire cavalry showed up, I explained the Cheerio phenomenon and that it was the Tai Chi Tao Pao in Emma who found the enlightened way. "Diana, your niece has skill," I said.

"Don't talk about her that way," Fannie said as she stepped inside behind Margie, Evan and Diana.

Diana grabbed Fannie at the collar and held her back. "Oh, shut up, Fannie. If you would shut up, maybe this little Emma could get a word in edgewise."

Tyler, the Mystic's bartender, knelt down beside Emma. "Wow, good for you. Now why don't you take this and go outside while we get Lexi out?" He handed her a dollar bill and she smiled.

Evan flexed his biceps. "Okay you ladies, out! Out while we pull these boards up. Nails will go flying."

Everyone stood outside the door while Evan and I pulled the boards up one at a time to reveal two black paws.

"Diana, come in here with your mystical hat and retrieve your dog," I said then hit Evan on the back. "Good work, for a guy."

Diana pulled her silvery salt-and-pepper hair back in a ponytail and got on her stomach and grabbed Lexi by the paws and pulled. "Come on girl. Bee Geez. I thought you were dead. I think you were going after that rabbit or maybe the groundhog. Come on girl. It's okay."

Lexi whined and slowly emerged with tattered and matted hair. Her scared pinched face relaxed as Anika pounced on her with two paws and licked her jaw, face and eyes. Once up, Lexi ran out of the shed and she and Anika bounded around like they hadn't seen each other in forty-nine dog years.

Then, from around the corner, the Antichrist showed up again—Fannie.

She shifted her red wig. "Leave my daughter alone, you little...you hear me. I don't care if your dad is going to be a custodian at the high school."

"What are you talking about? I'm not messing with Emma and Dad's not got a big super J on his chest or anything."

The surly bat looked from me to Margie then back to me. Emma peered around the corner.

"I'm just saying that this is the truth. That's all. Stay away from her."

Margie spoke up. "Fannie, we're not goofing around with your little girl. She's ten and eats Cheerios and is the biggest brainiac this town has seen in its elementary school since the birth of the Teton Mountains."

Fannie wiped her mouth, the lipstick smeared on her shirt, and addressed Margie. "Your mom is as good as dead if you don't get that man away from her. Emma, come closer, dear." Emma stood behind Fannie grabbing her hand for comfort and safety.

I exhaled a swirly smoke angel from my cigarette and said, "Whoa dude. Your wig is way too tight tonight, Fannie Why don't you just go back to your trailer and make some witch stew and throw in a few Cheerios. Just don't boil your daughter.

You're making this whole night get weirder than it's supposed to." I winked again at Emma. She seemed to smile even though I had thrown her in the stew.

Fannie came closer to me. "Keep your hands off my daughter. Or, I'll put that smoke ring so far up your butt you'll be blowing smoke dust out your face and ass for the next fifteen years."

Hand in hand, they walked away from the remnants of the outbuilding we'd just half leveled to get Lexi out.

"Beelzebub, what was that about?" Margie looked at the departing two figures, then at me, then stuffed her smokes back in her pocket.

"I have no planetary idea, Marge. Seems like the town psycho is far more babblier than we thought she might be. I feel sorry for her daughter. She's got the purest face I've ever seen."

Oneida was out of her vehicle and talking to a small group of people in front of the church when I arrived. It was 7:48 a.m. and I parked my Jeep next to hers. She had already put up a line of yellow tape so people wouldn't traipse all over the side grounds of the church. On the sidewalk, Raymond White pulled out a flask from his inside coat pocket. His hands shook as he took a swig. I walked toward him.

"Hey, Ray," I said. "How've you been?" Gauging that the temperature was about fifty or fifty-five degrees, I zipped up my jacket. My leather shoes squeaked and I put my hands deep into my pockets. I looked to Oneida's group and the outline of the church's apex, the wood, the glass, some stained, some not. Simple.

"Howdy, Blair. Pretty good. Pretty good." He took another swig and wiped his unshaven face with the back of his hand. Ray had a great book of knowledge on the goings on in the town square and all of the alleys behind every motel and restaurant. When Fannie wasn't around, Diana let him sleep in the outbuilding behind the *Mystic Market*. I liked him even though he'd assisted in Margie's mother's untimely death by screwing her into a heart attack in the alley behind the Cowboy Bar.

We stayed silent as we emerged more closely to the scene. Either a basketball player or student or someone from the Martinez family had put some pictures up on an easel toward the front door. There, a small cement marker held a metal crown of thorns lying in a state of ghastly repose upon it. I did not understand the image but then I looked at the statue closer to the door. It was of the Virgin Mary with her head down and her arms down with her palms facing up and outward. I got slightly dizzy.

Ray took one more swallow and turned to me with his ruddy face and dirty hands and he scratched his head. "You know what happened, I figure," he said, then internally belched.

"Yes. You?"

"Oh, yeah. I heard your dad yelling yesterday morning as I was going over toward the high school to do some foraging. Those kids are always leaving their coats or shoes or something. I stood at the corner of the gym and gave him a nip or two till the police showed up. Oneida there. See?"

"Yeah. I see." I patted him on the back. "You need anything, come by the Mystic and we'll help you out!"

"I'm going to live to be a hundred and thirty-five and die in my sleep," he said suddenly and without prompting.

"I thought it was a hundred and twenty-five, Ray?"

"I upped it. Need more time. Time and space and a good wormhole. Relativity."

For crying out loud, Ray was entering even more lunacy. I let it go and said, "Well, Einstein was definitely onto something."

"Was. Was. You mean is. Is onto something," Ray said then walked away muttering to himself.

"See you around, Ray," I said and meandered my way slowly over to Oneida.

Oneida stepped away from the few mourners that were there early this Sunday. Two students I recognized walked over with flowers and bowed heads toward the easel perched near the crown of thorns, their eyes blurry and red.

"You're late, Ms. Wingfield. You need some coffee? Father Mark has some set up in the front of the church in the foyer."

"Coffee, yes, but I'm a bit hesitant to go in there," I said, shuffling my shoes and lowering my head.

Oneida got her slam on. "Blair, what's up? You think Jesus is going to tackle you and put a leper Lazarus spell on you?"

My stomach longed for some Pepto-Bismol. "No, I just get an icky feeling when I go into churches, Oneida silverware."

"Shut it. Don't use that silverware shit with me. I'll bust your head wide open and lock you up in the jail with stinky Ray White."

We both looked up as he ambled around the block.

I said, "I'd rather be in jail with him than with you in there."

"Oh, for crying out loud. You're going to have to go in there because that's where Judd has asked the ballplayers to come in for their interviews. You're on the lead to talk to them, Blair." Oneida walked up the incline toward the church doors.

"Oneida. Stop. Stop." She ignored me with a back of the hand in the air.

"Get your bony atheist ass in here. A girl is dead. This is not about how you feel about Christianity or any religion. It's about her, dumbass."

Under my breath, I said, "Why does everyone think this is about me?"

"When are they coming?"

"Who?" She opened the front glass door. I quickly peered at the easel of Mary Louise and scanned the six or seven onlookers. I recognized a few men from Aaron's poker game and the others were some Hispanic-looking girls and guys all huddled together like they were in a prayer scrum.

"The players?"

"Judd went by the coach's house last night and asked us to interview the coach and the players one at a time. There's twelve total. Thirteen if you count the manager. So it may take most of today and tomorrow. I have no idea who will interview Susie Clarkson. I think Judd and Todd will do her. There's a vigil service here tonight at seven p.m. Family is making arrangements today."

I walked through the doors into the threshold. The foyer was lit, but the sanctuary was not. Oneida ambled over to get some coffee. I watched her in seeming slow motion as I began for whatever reason to feel dizzy in my head again. I removed my deputy ball cap and looked back outside to the people who had brought flowers. Down the street a bit, I saw several small groups showing up for the same purpose: to pay homage to a young, bright woman.

As I looked back to Oneida, something deep in the breadth of my being forced me to rotate my head and eyes into the sanctuary. The double doors leading to it were open, and without hesitation I took four delicate steps to the doorway. I took my left hand from my pocket and placed it on the frame of the door. As I peered into the sanctuary, the hollow holy house, my eyes traced the pews to the left, the pews to the right—the hokey pokey. I smiled in amusement. When my eyes got to the altar, for some odd reason, I looked up and suspended from the ceiling was a giant Jesus on the cross, the martyr, the crucified Holy Man. He was hanging. A nail in his left hand to a board, a nail on his right hand to a board, his feet one over the other and nailed to a third board. On his head a crown of thorns, his head down.

The crystalline flash of Mary Louise Martinez superimposed over him. It flashed one, two, three times. The vomit came to my throat, my hand went to my neck.

I fell, face forward and nearly knocked out a tooth on the first pew. I landed on both knees and held my body against the wood of the pew momentarily till I could jar myself out of it.

I'd heard of foreshadowing and signs, but this was ridiculous.

CHAPTER SIX

The media did not show up as Judd had thought. Too early a news item, we all speculated. The local news did stop by and take a statement from Judd that aired later that night. You could see Oneida and me in the background standing on guard in front of the church. It was my first cameo on TV and Aaron typed into his keyboard, "You. Look. Very. Official. Mom. Would. Be. Proud. That. You. Look. Like. You. Are. Guarding. A. Church." He laughed and some drool came out and I gave him the finger.

Several days later Emma Jacobs came like a whirling dervish into the Mystic Market to speak to her mother. It had been since before college that I'd encountered Emma in the Mystic and I was surprised to see her suddenly appear that late March evening. Her green North Face jacket was unzipped and her legs muscular inside the tailored jeans and brown shoes. I looked out the front window to see the red Dodge Dakota with Evan sitting in it, holding his small Christian vigil. Squinting at him, I unveiled an evil internal mantra that involved Gabriel, the biting cat, clawing him on his ass in the middle of the night and attacking his early phallic riser with a clawed paw before he made it to the bathroom. My stomach again grew green with envy and I held it in with a long-drawn-out breath and a sip of beer. Emma saw me sitting at the counter in my street clothes: jeans, Timberland boots and a long-sleeve flannel shirt. A dyke's uniform; a dyke in waiting.

"Hey, Blair," Emma tossed over to me and then went over to Diana who was doing trigonometry with her Excel spreadsheet and bills. All that woman did was worry about money. In the derailed economy, I understood why.

"Emma. How goes it with the practice?" I asked. I wanted her to come and talk to me, so I swung around on my barstool and waited for an answer. Nothing. I waited. Still nothing. Emma sat down next to Diana and started small talk I could not hear. I looked out the window at Evan sitting in the truck and hoped that he was good to her. Come on Gabriel, you can do it boy. I smiled and swallowed some beer.

Fannie came out of the back room and right over to me. "Did you read about the unveiled mysteries? Did you read about them?"

"What are you talking about, Fannie?" I asked, then looked at her eye to eye, tired of her nonsensical Dadaism. Her face took on a tiredness and her hair was slightly unkempt. She fiddled and shuffled her Tarot cards in her hands. Looking up from her conversation with Emma, Diana regarded Fannie with a semblance of sisterly love that only came with the line of blood between them. Looking at Diana, I could see where Emma got her large Yale brain. Looking at Fannie, I could see where Emma got her creative spark for writing.

"Pick a card," Fannie suddenly demanded of me.

"Fannie, you never ask me to pick a card. Why now?"

Emma came over quickly to intercept and stood next to the two of us.

Fannie kept looking at me. "Just pick a card, Blair. How hard is it? Jesus!"

"Mom, come on. Diana said you're not getting enough sleep since Mary Louise died. Come on. Let Evan and me take you home. We'll watch a movie or make you some dinner." Emma put her hand on mine then quickly retracted it.

"You can cook, Emma?" I asked, and then slid my hand on top of the deck of cards. Fannie seemed to enjoy this.

When Emma's sultry blue eyes landed on me, it was clear I needed to pick a card and let the sexual wash I was having clean my ass up. I couldn't believe it. Emma Jacobs was giving me a vibe. Her body was next to five or so inches from mine and her mom was shoving a stack of cards my way, but whoa Nelly, I do believe this time she was actually giving me some sort of sexual vibration. My body was aquiver and I gracefully knocked over the stack of cards Fannie was holding out for me. The entire village of the Tarot fell all over the floor and then something very odd happened. Fannie burbled up some vomit and before we could get her to the bathroom, she puked all over the floor. Diana ran over from her perch and grabbed the other side of her sister. I hung back and looked back out to see if Evan was still holding vigil. He was. Tush.

Then I looked down at the floor. I knew nothing about Tarot cards or Mystics or sage or incense or auras or chakras or anything. I read sporting magazines and went to rock concerts. I did not cook, nor did I care to. I knew about my brother's ailments and I understood depression to the extent that I had taken a pill or two on occasion to help with the winter doldrums. I reached down to pick up the cards and pulled one up to look at it. At the bottom, it said Wheel of Fortune. It made me think of Pat Sajak and Vanna White.

Emma emerged from the back and came over to me.

"Blair, for some reason, she really wants you back there. She's really upset."

I handed Emma the Tarot card. She glanced at it then knelt down on the ground to pick up what I had missed.

"Why me, Emma? This is strange."

"Evidently she thinks you have some strange power that will help resurrect the girl who died."

I stared at Emma.

"Mary Louise Martinez. She says she's been dreaming about you for the last four or five days and it's gotten her upset. Can you talk to her, Blair?"

Her voice was so soft, so subtle for such a rock hard brainiac.

The scourge of Fannie Crabwell was upon me. We'd always hated each other and done arcs of survival around the Mystic Market to stay out of each other's way. I shoved my hands in my pockets and slowly walked toward the back where Fannie was in her small psychic reading room. It smelled like sandalwood and vanilla and there were tiny rocks and gems scattered about her table. Fannie sat at her table and had her head in her hands and Diana was rubbing her back as I stood there holding back the curtain.

"I'll leave you two alone for a few minutes," Diana said. "I need to go out back and check on my new puppy. Have you seen her, Blair?"

I couldn't stop looking at Fannie who just sat there hunched and catatonic. I felt breathy. "No, I haven't seen a puppy."

"Well, she's really about six months old. Judy Dixon from over at the sheriff's department found her by the Snake last week, down near Piney Woods. Doesn't look like she's eaten in three months. She's a scrawny thing. Come out back when you get a chance."

"I will."

Fannie looked up at me and then put her head back in her hands. "You can sit. It's no big deal. Maybe I'm wrong. Have you read the unveiled mysteries? The discourses about Godfre Ray King?"

I sat and tersely said, "No. Fannie, I haven't read those books. I'm just doing my job for Teton County and going to work every day and trying to take care of Aaron. You know that."

"How is the king of drool doing?"

"You know, Fannie, I was half expecting something different here between you and me. But, I guess not." I stood up.

"In my past life regression, I know I was a killer," Fannie said suddenly. "I wasn't anyone special like Sacagawea or, hell, Lewis and Clark. I killed things. I may have killed people. Now I've been brought about with the disease in my brain. But I still love. I still love things and only some sorts of people. I liked her. The girl who died." Fannie put her head in her hands again. "I didn't know who she was or that she might be queer like you."

"How would you have known?" I cocked my head to the side and felt a presence behind me but did not turn.

"She helped me one day at Jackson Drug. Some kids were making fun of me in the back. I could hear them under their collective asshole breaths saying I was the town crazy. Then one of them jumped in front of me and shouted 'Boo'. They all started laughing and then Mary Louise Martinez came over from the candy aisle. I remember she had her little sister or brother with her. I couldn't tell because it was winter and the little cherub was tied up like a papoose. At any rate, she started speaking in Spanish to two of the kids and then she shoved the 'boo' person in the shoulder."

"Wow," I said. "Sounds like she was taking up for you, eh?"

"No one does. No one takes up for me. She walked me out the side door of the store and up to the square. She asked me if I was okay. She asked me if I was okay." Her voice became shrill, then she said it one more time shrillier and louder. "She asked me if I was okay."

"Mom!" Emma brushed by me and went to her mother. "Let's go. Blair, can you help me with her to the door?"

"I don't understand any of this," I said. "Why are you so upset?"

Emma said nothing as she helped her mother up. "I'm taking the case, Blair. I'm going to need to talk with you and the other deputies who took responses from the students." Emma said this as we all began our walk down the center aisle of the market.

"Okay," I said dumbly. Then I asked, "What case, Emma?"

"I talked with Mr. Martinez and Mary Louise's uncle yesterday. Evidently, they found a box of notes in the back of her closet. She was having an affair, Blair."

"With who?" I asked. "I can't believe it."

Then Emma mouthed the words. I shook my head.

Finally, at the front door, I opened it for them. "It rhymes with roach, Blair. Roach."

"Oh my," I said. "This is deplorable. We're going to need that evidence."

Emma got outside and ushered her mother to the truck.

"About time!" barked Evan from the front seat.

Just then, Diana came around with a scrawny German shepherd. "Hey, you guys. Meet Jackson Hole's newest member of the Mystic Market."

"What's her name, Diana?" I asked.

"Maya, like Maya Angelou," she said. The dog was wagging all over the place and her shoulder blades were poking from her skin. Scout, her chocolate lab rescue, nuzzled her all over.

"Keep that scrawny wombat away from me," Fannie said as she climbed in the truck. Emma closed the door and came over to pet Maya.

"Hey, Maya." Emma leaned down. "You're so sweet. Look at you. Look at you. Awwww. Diana," she cooed as she continued to rub the dog's head and fur, "she's beautiful."

I leaned over to pet Maya too, and then squatted down to get eye to eye with her. Her dark brown eyes seemed to wink at me and my heart went aflutter.

Momentarily, in the petting of Maya, Emma's hand brushed against mine and I regarded her just like when we were just in the market. She regarded me too, for a second, then looked up at Diana. The slip. She gave me the slip. Something was there, and the Deputy Fife in me was on it.

"Diana," she said, "I think you've got a winner here."

"I know now you're talking about me. The coolest deputy sheriff this side of Idaho." I smiled and then put my hands in the air as if signaling a touchdown.

Emma giggled. "You're the coolest sheriff only because you take care of that sweet brother of yours. He's quite the poet, you know!"

"Yeah, I keep telling him he needs to write that bestseller so we can both retire."

Diana knelt down and held the new puppy in her arms and lavished her with love. "Well, maybe we can all retire soon. This latest tragedy has about killed me. The whole town is in mourning. Everyone's wearing black and Mary Louise's basketball number on something. Ten. Such a transformational number. Such a good kid. Ten. Like she was perfect." The tears welled up in Diana's eyes. "I still can't believe it. And your mother, Emma—it's gotten her knickers all in veritable twist."

"I know. I know. Evan and I are going to take her home and get her distracted somehow." Emma stood and zipped her jacket.

"How did you manage to come out the way you did, Emma? With a crazy wig worm of a mother like that and a sane pillar of support like Diana?" I stood up.

Emma stood up. We were face to face. I thought for a second that she would say something, anything, as I'd incited her kindly to do so. But she didn't. She hugged her aunt and patted the dog and then climbed in the truck.

The truck pulled away and Maya was whining for more pets. "How did she manage, Diana?" I asked.

Diana regarded the mountain, the sky and then me. "She's got the purest heart of anyone I've ever met. Her brain is teeming with words and thoughts and phrases but she rarely tells you what she thinks. She likes to keep it inside; all tied up like it keeps her company or something."

We both turned to the front of the Mystic Market. Diana adjusted her scarf and put her arm around me. Her arm felt sweet and good.

"After the funeral tomorrow, Blair, I'm going to have some people over to the market. You want to stop by after you leave the church?"

"I'm not going to the church. I'm taking Aaron, but I'm not going."

"Okay. Good. Church sucks sometimes. You can help me here. I've decided to have my favorite local guitar lady come and sing."

"You mean, Amy Henderson?"

"Absolutely…she kicks butt and I think it will be good to have some music and some people here."

"I'm in. Is Fannie going to be around?"

"Of course. Emma will too. She's taking the case against Teton County Schools it looks like. The Martinez family has asked her."

"Diana? Are they getting married?"

"Evan and Emma? Not if she doesn't kick his sorry ass out first. The ungrateful angry bastard."

"How do you really feel about him?"

She smiled and I smiled and I walked up toward my bungalow. In the distance, I heard music but could not tell from which bungalow it came, mine or someone else's. My heart was heavy and Fannie had made me feel jumpy but that was okay. My body was beginning to have its own personal awakening every time Emma Jacobs showed her face. She was younger than I was... but not too much younger. The demon in me swelled up and I longed suddenly to be in her presence again, to be in her arms, to be kissing. Twisted. I was twisted for sure.

And straight girls were always trouble.

CHAPTER SEVEN

The entire town of Jackson Hole seemed to shut itself down for the funeral of Mary Louise Martinez. The school district held elementary school classes only. The funeral service was at eleven o'clock in the morning and I had to help with parking and traffic at Our Lady of the Mount. We created off-street parking nearby at the rodeo grounds and many people walked two or three blocks to the church. Several elderly parishioners held the doors open and Aaron and Emma and Evan all went in together. Evan was wearing cowboy boots, a denim shirt with a tie and I secretly tied him to a tree or a rock and left him there like Prometheus for stealing what was becoming my mythic fire. Why I momentarily managed that image, I did not know.

Dirty Ray White came to the sidewalk where I completed my tiny missions in moving cones and directing traffic as people in their black mourning outfits came to pay their respects to a basketball star, an honors student, a lesbian.

What I didn't expect to see was a news van that I didn't recognize. I knew that we had made some waves in Jackson and nearby towns with her death, but I wasn't ready to see a national news outlet come down the street. The driver rolled his window down and waved me over.

"We're from a Fox news affiliate in Colorado," he said. "Can we park our truck here and set up a camera on the sidewalk in front of the church?"

I stumbled for a second. The hair went up on the back of my neck, razor-like. Peering in the van, I saw equipment and a woman dressed up and with more makeup than I'd ever seen. "Yes, park a block down. You can set up your equipment at the south end of the church over there." I pointed, dumbly.

"Thanks," he said and pulled his van away slowly and I looked over at Dirty Ray.

"Looks like trouble," he said and swigged from his flask.

And, it was. Ten minutes later, another news van showed up. This one was local but behind it was a car that had people I'd never seen in it. They stopped.

"Hey, deputy," the woman said from her window. "We're setting up for a news conference taking place after the funeral. Can we park here?"

Dumbly, I pointed again.

"More trouble," Ray said and sat on the curb.

"What's going on?" I asked.

Just then, Oneida and Sheriff Williams came toward my side of the street. Oneida held a clipboard and Judd walked with an awkward cowboy gait as if he'd ridden too many bulls. Oneida looked at me and shook her head in a quiet warning.

Judd took his hands out of his jacket pockets and looked at Ray. Ray quickly put his flask away. Out of the corner of my eye, I saw my father walk toward the church. He glanced our way. I waved slightly and returned my gaze to the tower of a man before me.

Judd cleared his throat and looked up to the sky. "Looks like we're getting some media attention, Blair. I'm going to hold a press conference after the funeral today and discuss the particulars of the suicide. Someone has leaked to the press some news that is going to put the Teton County school system in a gray light. What I already suspected."

I looked questioningly at Oneida who had a furrowed brow. She pulled out a cigarette and lit up. Ray got up and sidewindered over to where he could listen.

I played as if I hadn't talked to Emma already. "What's the news, Judd? I thought it was a closed case. Suicide. That's all."

He ignored my question as usual. "Blair, I want you to help with the people who have contacted us from the Human Rights Campaign. They need a law enforcement contact and I want it to be you. It's not a closed case. Evidently, there were some notes, er, letters from Coach Palonski to Mary Louise. Mary Louise wrote some too. Her parents found them in a shoebox in the back of her closet."

"What was in them?" I asked, again holding in the fact I'd already spoken to Emma. I whistled like a bird for another car to move toward the side lot.

Oneida exhaled. "They were having an affair. We think Coach Palonski recently broke it off after her husband caught wind."

"Holy homosexual hellions," I said, feigning surprise. "Palonski, I always thought her hair and jaw were too square and her gait mighty manly."

Judd waved at some passersby as they went into the church. "Emma Jacobs is going to represent the Martinez family. They've already hired her. Virgil Steele will defend the school system. It's gotten heated already and the girl isn't even in the ground yet."

For the second time in a week, I wanted to fall on my knees again. My hands felt like they were on fire and I clenched my butt cheeks together to form some sort of opinion on the matter.

"Judd. Oneida. I think Coach Palonski has two kids, right?"

"She does," Oneida said. "From what I see it won't be long before our sheriff here is on *The Today Show*, *Good Morning America* and CNN. This makes the case a hotbed for the media and we've got to be ready."

I stepped back and hailed a car into the parking area. I waved them in and then watched an eagle land on its thick bird feet looking for some carrion close by. Ah, Prometheus. Your great eagle has arrived to eat out your liver. "I will talk to the Human Rights people, Judd. But I don't want to talk to the media. If my mom sees me on TV, then she'll fly up here in a heartbeat. I don't want that."

Oneida laughed. "She'll want to be on TV herself. Mrs. Florida Gator."

Judd turned and began to walk away. "Let's meet after the press conference at the office with the other officers and with the Jackson police. I've already spoken to the producers at *Good Morning America*, by the way. They called me last night. We need to be ready for any demonstrations or any backlash from the Christian Right. It's probably coming sooner than we think."

"Didn't you vote for Bush, Judd?" I asked.

"I did, Blair, but it doesn't mean I'm an asshole. Not all Republicans are awful as many Democrats want to believe."

I considered his quick retort. "I don't think you're an asshole, Judd. Just a Republican nimrod with a heart. How's that?"

"Better. You still want your job, right?"

"Nah, you can give my shift to Oneida. I'd rather be at home taking care of Aaron and tubing on Cache Creek."

"It won't be long, Blair. And, bite my ass."

Oneida put her hands up. "Stop it, you two. We've got a funeral going on here. You all should be behaving better than this."

"Okay," Judd said, and asked, "What should I say, Oneida?"

"You should say a prayer for both of your sorry asses," she said, then exhaled smoke, dropped her cigarette to the ground, punched it out with her polished shoe and retrieved the butt for her pocket.

We all giggled. Ray did, too—a moment of relief from the building tension.

"Don't forget, Blair. You're on escort in front of the pack. Oneida and me and seven officers from Jackson police are flanking. Marty is on rear post." Judd audibly exhaled.

Clouds had formed over the mountains in all directions from

town. For a moment, the three of us turned and looked toward the church. It was as if we were all looking up for an answer to the sudden shock and awe of the events of the last week. When I scanned the crowd, I saw Mary Louise Martinez's mother and father walking as if shackled together in despair entering the church, the cloak of their sadness deeper than any indigo of any night I'd ever seen in the bucolic place I lived. The two brothers and the sister of the fallen student trailed behind them in order of their ages. The twin brothers looked about fifteen and their sister about ten.

I put my hand on my stomach and felt it turn somersaults. Students from Teton High School moved in synchronized slow motion, everyone with bowed heads, holding hands, tissues up to their noses.

Oneida quietly eked out, "It's the worst to lose a family member. We need to try and honor those people with the work we do here."

"Just remember. The school board, superintendent and principal of Teton High School are getting ready to go on very public trial," Judd added.

Then I said quietly, "For a very private behavior. It's not like they are involved in a hate crime where it's the color of your skin or your religion or your ethnicity or belief system. It's the most personal of all. What's in between one's legs. Right, Judd?"

"Exactly."

Then Oneida corrected me. "Come on Blair. This *is* a hate crime. She hated herself enough to do it. Just like those bullied teenagers from last fall. All hanging, jumping and shooting themselves to death. It's insane."

The memorial service lasted for an hour and I stayed with the passersby in the whipping wind while the ceremony went on. In my mind's eye, I imagined some students and perhaps a sibling making comments on the eighteen years Mary Louise Martinez was on this planet. An open casket and makeup to hide the marks on her neck. I spat on the ground in disgust hoping no one saw, but then I didn't care. My cells were turning red from resentment at the cancerous poison of the hate speech that characterized the schools all over America, all over the world.

An emptiness crept into my hollow heart. Who are we? Who am I? What is all of this for?

By the time the mourners began the processional from the church, I was in my deputy's Jeep with the lights on in front of the hearse. Once the casket was pushed into the back, I had to wait nearly twenty-five minutes for the two hundred or so people to get in their cars or begin the walk. Since Jackson was such a small town, and with Mary Louise suddenly becoming such a major player in the gay rights movement, the anti-bullying movement, perhaps this was a hopeful in a movement to end all LGBT movements. Buses to Birmingham, perhaps? Or, like Martin Luther King, we were all falling on the right side of history. Or at least we hoped. She was the newest casualty in the plea to stop. Stop the Biblical madness once and for all. The Old Testament, Oneida had once said to me, was killing gay people still. The New Testament wasn't much better but at least Jesus was on our side. When she had brought it all up, I told her to shut it. Shut it down. I knew the Bible had those places like in Luke counting the dumbass hairs and or that marketing director fool, Paul, who wrote way too many letters and should have been counting his stupid blessings instead. God, counting again. At least I could count on my Gnosticism.

I blipped my siren on and off once as we pulled out of the church. Since the cemetery was not far away, the Martinez family had asked if we could travel in a wide circle around town then pass town square before making it to Aspen Hill Cemetery. I obliged and was glad that many people had come to line the streets. My heart sank as I passed the Fred Phelps Westboro Church of Satan and its eight or nine missionaries who held signs up that said, "*Mary Louise Meets Matthew in Hell.*" I suddenly blared my siren as I passed them and scared two of them into hitting the ground. Fuck you.

When we got to the cemetery at the bottom of Snow King Mountain, I shut my lights off and got out in case any protestors showed up to fling their flapping jibber at a very pained and saddened family and town. I watched as the pallbearers led her casket to the plot. Father Mark solemnly began to speak. Out of the corner of my eye, I watched my brother put his hands together in prayer as Emma stood by him, Diana and Fannie. My brother believed. He never talked of it with me. But, he believed in God. He believed in prayer. On occasion, I'd heard him at night whispering short repetitive prayers with his hands on his head. Mainly, prayerful pleas. I shut the door when I heard him do it.

An hour later, Father Mark allowed a short press conference to be held outside of the church. Reporters wrangled with microphones and cameras and pen and paper to ask Judd questions about the suicide and the impending court case. Judd dismissed leading questions and kept it to the facts. He named Emma and Virgil as attorneys who would be taking the case. For the entire conference, I could not focus at all. I was physically dizzy and had to steady myself on a pew. Image after image of Mary Louise haunted my mind—her body hanging. The contents of the note, a mystery.

After my shift, I went by the office to pick up some CDs I'd left in my desk. I felt the need to take a ride around the town and perhaps up toward Teton Pass. The driving would allow me to think and I could seek some solitude in the countryside. Before I could even get out onto the main highway, I saw a car weaving to the left and then weaving all over the road. I called in the tag, hit the lights and pulled the car over. Momentarily, I did not recognize the heavily made up woman in the front seat, but then she surfaced in my mind: Carleen Proust, the cheerleader I would have liked to have kissed in high school. Sitting shotgun was Evan Adams, Emma's live-in boyfriend. Right away, I was pissed off and could barely contain myself. I smelled alcohol and did the usual: waited for the suspect to give it away.

"Why officer, what did I do?" came Carleen's response. Then she recognized me. "Oh, hey, Blair. How are you? Lord girl it's been a while. What did I do wrong?"

"You went over the line several times, ma'am," I said. "I mean Carleen."

Evan leaned forward.

"Sir, can you please lean back so I can see your hands," I declared.

Evan laughed. "I think you know who I am, Blair."

"Evan, I'm just following the rules. Do you want to play or get into trouble?"

"You sure are sassy," he said then leaned back.

I ignored his retort and asked Carleen for her driver's license and registration. "Stay here, I'll be right back."

I went back to my vehicle fuming and tripped at the front of my Jeep. I could hear Evan laughing and could feel the Barney Fife in me getting all flared up. I radioed in that I was doing a potential DUI stop and asked for a second car to come out.

When I returned to the vehicle, Carleen had her hand on Evan's thigh. She removed it quickly.

"Did you go to the funeral today, deputy?" Evan asked. "Such a horrible thing to happen to a lesbian."

"I think it's a horrible thing to happen to anyone, lesbian or not." I felt like I was giving myself away.

"I was just driving this young man home, officer. He's the one who can't drive." Carleen smiled at me like I was two.

"How much have you had to drink?"

"Me? None. I've had none. I was probably swerving a bit 'cause this cutie here was makin' me laugh so hard. I didn't even see you from behind."

Just then our oldest deputy on the force showed up. Frank Jones. He stayed in his car and gave me a slight wave. I wished he'd have gotten out but saw he was eating a sandwich, probably playing Scrabble on his Droid. Our tax dollars always hard at work.

Carleen did her ABC's fine and when I asked her to step out of the car, she thought it was the funniest thing ever. I saw no humor in it and kept glancing at Evan-the-cheater Adams. Her lipstick was smeared across her face and I couldn't wait to get away from the scene of this crime and tell Emma. Jesus.

Suddenly, Evan got out of the car. He was pissed.

"Blair, leave her alone. I'm the one who's had a few too many." He slurred his words a bit and his eyes were red.

Deputy Jones got on his intercom and dolefully said, "Get back into the vehicle. Get back into the vehicle. Now!"

On the word, "now," Evan slowly got back into the car. His surly demeanor trailed itself with him as he slammed the door.

I had her do several tests to establish her drunkenness and when she passed the walking test, I decided to make her blow anyway, just to be sure. As I held the breathalyzer to her mouth and asked her to blow, she winked at me as if it were all a big joke and I accidentally dropped it to the ground.

Officer Jones got out of his car and wiped his mouth clean as I continued my nervousness in trying to establish the drunken woman. Emma's eyes flashed into my mind's eye and I could only imagine her disgust when I told her about my fortuitous traffic stop.

I asked Carleen to get back in the car. Back at my vehicle, I ran the plate and tags and checked her insurance. Everything was in order. I struggled with my radio and called in that I was letting her go. Her blood alcohol was below the legal limit. I went back to the vehicle and saw that Evan was giggling and flirting with Carleen-the-whore Proust.

"Go ahead and get him home, Ms. Proust. Drive more carefully. I'm just letting you go with a verbal warning."

"Slice her up with your words, Blair. Give her a bitch slap. I'd love to see it," Evan said and snickered.

"Evan, I can still write you up. You were drunk in public somewhere before you got into this car." I handed Carleen her ID and registration.

Walking away, I overheard Carleen say, "What's gotten up her twat?" Then Evan said, "She needs a dick to calm her ass down!"

I almost went back and arrested him but was too tired from the funeral, the press conference and the heaviness of the day. And all I could see and feel was Emma. *Dumbass Evan*, I thought. *Republican dumbass Tea Party right wing dickhead.*

I hailed Deputy Jones away and got back in my Jeep. Maybe I should get into the K-9 unit and just do drug busts. I hated traffic stops as you never knew what you were getting into. At least with a dog, there was safety and no judgment.

Carleen and Evan drove off into the Wyoming sunset.

I felt an opening in the hole of my soul.

I headed at high speed straight to Emma's house on Hansen Street. When I got there, there was a note on the door. Evan's name plastered on the front. No sign of Emma. I dared not open the envelope but my nosiness got the best of me. Emma's disdain was apparent, I noted quickly:

Evan,
Gone to the Mystic Market with my mom. Please don't come. You can do whatever you want. You do so anyway.
Emma

Ouch. The evidence was clear.

I sailed to the Mystic checking my chin hairs in the mirror, remembering there would be music and Mary Louise Martinez mourners littering the place with snot, why's and how could this happens? I felt similarly but mainly was feeling a draw to Emma I'd never felt before. I would tell her about the traffic stop. No. I couldn't tell her. I didn't know what I would do. I had to get to Aaron. Maybe he could help.

I pulled into a spot near our bungalow which was set in the woods of an outpost of Cache Creek winding its way around a bend in the historic rock and grass. My gaze fell on Maya, the new large puppy, barking at Ray White who was trying his best to walk into the outbuilding we'd freed the old dog from many years earlier. He was shushing the dog and laughing at the same time. Maya lay on the ground hoping he'd make a move that would allow her to pounce on him.

"Come here, Maya Angelou!" I yelled at the dog. She looked at me like I had three heads. I called again. "It's just Ray, Maya. It's okay. Come here girl." I leaned down on one knee and by the time Maya had come over to me, Emma was outside in a long dark coat cloaking her in the spring weather and the setting sun.

Ray tipped his head and flask my way. I patted Maya on her head, then rubbed her ears till she began to jiggle one of her back legs.

"Blair, you have a way with dogs. How are you?" she asked rhetorically. I could sense the inherent sadness in the shadows of her face.

"Maya here is very sweet. I was just thinking about serving

in the K-9 unit a little while ago when I was on patrol. Um. Have you seen Aaron?" I felt nervous and looked down. I kept patting Maya, hoping the poetic dog would help.

"He's in there. You okay?"

"Yeah, why?" I asked.

Maya rolled over on her back and showed her belly and then did a dog dance on her backside getting in a scratch. Her wiggling amused us both.

Emma stepped closer. "You look a bit tired. That uniform of yours is sagging on you." She was genuinely worried about me. Something I hadn't had someone do in a long time. Worry about me. What in the world?

I laughed. "You think? It's a bit big but I'm eating more protein bars to help fill me out a little. How is everyone doing in there?" I nodded toward the Mystic.

"How can anything be right when a teenager takes her own life? The Martinez family is verifiably paralyzed in their state of mourning. The mother barely speaks and the father just drinks whiskey all day and all night. The kids are where kids are when tragic things happen."

"Where's that?" I asked.

"In the palm of the Lord's hand." She said it with such ease and grace and lightness that I thought my dentures would fly from my mouth.

"Yes, he's usually got his arm and palm very extended. Especially last Saturday morning when he was there to give his holy palm a hand to Mary Louise as she tied a knot around her neck and kicked over a ladder." I said this with the kind of disdain and animosity I'd felt my whole life for the vacant God of my dreams, nightmares and life.

"Blair, I didn't know you felt this way." Emma put her hands in her coat pockets and came closer. I stepped back out of a bit of fear.

"I saw Evan today," I blurted.

"Yeah, was he with his new girlfriend?"

"You know?" I asked.

"The signs were everywhere. But I guess you don't do signs, Blair, since you don't believe in God."

"A simple agnostic slash atheist—depending on my mood and what has happened." I asked, "What signs?"

"Well, we've been together off and on for a long time. He drinks too much. There's one. He lies when the truth would be a better fit...even on the little things. But, when he asks me how he looks, asks me how his shirt looks—I knew then and there he was up to no good. I only let him sit with me in church today because he asked. He ditched the funeral for a beer and his new thing. It's been going on for quite some time. I've just been too busy with all of this to kick him out."

"You knew he was cheating?"

"Yep. Come on, Deputy. You've been doing this gig for a while. You know how to prove and solve the mysteries of people, places and things. I've been learning about criminal activity and behavior for a while now that I've taken on a litigious nature in my life."

"Litigious?" I asked, uncertain of its meaning.

"The law, Blair."

"Oh, yeah, right. Litigious. I'm not used to the sudden onset of big words, Ms. Yale Graduate Mensa Mind."

"Here, I thought I was the one who flaps words in the wind. And, I do believe you just mocked your own dexterity with the word Mensa Deputy. Mensa, really?" She smiled wide and strong.

Then the warmth between my legs spread. Did she just flirt with me? I did like a good word but the mockery made my hair tingle. What word would she use next?

There was a slight pause as I looked to the front of the Market where I could hear the lulling sound of Amy's guitar and the scratchiness of her voice singing out to the crowd. "Emma, do you want to go back in with me and have some coffee?"

"Sure. Do you think Maya will eat up Ray White if you're not out here?"

"Maya is a good girl. She's just not used to Ray yet. I bet in a week, we'll find them both in there where I saw you drop Cheerios once trying to lure your aunt's old dog out. Remember that old story? Ancient times, eh?"

"You and Margie were so cute. I used to look up to you all so much growing up. Oh my!" Emma turned to walk back to the Market. I sidled up next to her feeling kind of goofy that I was still in my uniform even though I was off duty.

"You looked up to us geeks?" I questioned. "We were so doofy and silly and stupid with everything."

"I was always in the Mystic with Mom and you guys were always coming in and talking about and sneaking about and you, you were the only one who always came over and played a game with me. Checkers." Emma put her hand on my back. "Thank you for that. And, yes, it does feel old and ancient, like home or something. I don't know."

I was reeling. "Yes. I remember when you graduated to chess when you were in high school, I couldn't keep up. You always got my queen. I finally gave up and we just did puzzles, remember? We did one huge one of a sailboat by a dock that had so much white in it. God, do you remember that?" I asked hoping she'd keep her hand where it was.

"Yes. That one and the one that had the woman with the red dress out by the red barn. That one was really hard. You got the cow and stopped." Emma slid her hand down my back as we neared the door. My nipples decided to shoot themselves into my bra.

"Lord," I exhaled and opened the door for her like a good woman in uniform should. Together, we walked into the Mystic and I glanced at my brother stealing the show by playing his electric keyboard and drooling all over himself.

"You're calling on the right party as my mom would say." Emma laughed and I laughed and for a fleeting second I felt normal. Okay, all right—just not so damn tight.

When the news came on that night, I saw that everything had gone viral. Mary Louise's name, her suicide, her sexuality. Flog her, I thought. Flog her some more. Get that lesbian.

Emma saw and felt the same. I felt it in my deep heart's core.

CHAPTER EIGHT

Two months later in early June, Margie Hostetler showed up just as the trial was to begin. When I opened the door, I met Mick. Mick was about four foot five and was almost a midget; her arms and legs weren't bowed—normal but tiny. Margie and Mick were buds and Mick was into rock and roll. She was an agent who dealt with some up-and-coming bands out in L.A. and she was always looking for a good time.

I put them up in the bungalow three doors down.

"Are. You. Working. Another. Long. Shift. Today?" Aaron asked me as he motored to the kitchen, his head cocked to one side. I saw his burgeoning manuscript tucked inside his motor home, all tattered at the edges.

"Yes. I. Am!" I smiled at him and then walked behind him and put my hands on his shoulders. He relaxed a bit. I rifled through the fridge foraging for some orange juice. I poured some into his plastic container holding a long straw he could lean into, and I poured a giant glass for myself.

Then Marge and Mick sashayed into the doorway of my bungalow both looking like they'd eaten the canary—smug, semi-salacious and funky. Terms of endearment.

"Knock, knock, you two retarded gay rods of nim." Not much had changed with Margie. Her hair was longer and she reeked of California coolness.

"Hey, Blair," Mick called to me. "Good morning to the Jackson prison bitch!" She laughed and I crossed my eyes at her. Our high school stupidity felt like an SNL sketch and I liked it.

"Hey, Mick. What are you doing with the Californicator of the century and pot dealer posing poetic?"

Margie laughed and came in through the door. "We're taking Aaron into town today to drink beer, play poker and deal crack to the school children. Will you be patrolling the area? Because Mick here loves to be cuffed up."

"That's a bit too much information. I gotta get to work then I'll meet you at the Mystic for some dinner then I'm off all weekend to play. Oneida wants to meet you Mick, so I think she may be tagging along." I ran back into my bedroom for my sheriff's hat. I grabbed a hat that said, 'CAP,' for Aaron and put it on his head as I ran back in. A birthday gift for him a month earlier.

Mick sat right next to Aaron and fiddled with his keyboard. Momentarily, I thought Aaron might not want her touching his keyboard, but he seemed to like the attention. I looked at Margie, she looked at me and winked. Christ. This must have been Margie's attempt at getting Aaron laid. Who knew her covert ops?

"What's on your cop agenda today, Ms. Deputy Dildo?" Margie asked.

"Okay, Margie, you can stop with the grinding epithets of doom. We're not in high school anymore," I said and buttoned the top of my brown shirt.

"Oh my, when did you get so tight, Blair Witch Trial? Eh? I think Deputy Dildo is a fine term for you." Margie swished back her large brown landscape of hair and grabbed a coffee mug.

Margie giggled. "Hey, Mick, one time when we were little,

Blair had an imaginary Jesus friend. Yeah—she killed him over at my house after she was cut from the girls' basketball team in sixth grade. It was a pivotal point in our inconsequential lives. Then, as an added bonus, she killed Jesus in an imaginary toothpick battle at the kitchen table and flushed him and the toothpick down the toilet."

I laughed in the moment. "Then," I added, "Satan came alive to me in a seriously good way when I was introduced to cigarettes, alcohol, wedgies and pot by your ashramic leader here." I pointed to Marge then grabbed a piece of paper that flew from Aaron's mobile home.

After fiddling with Aaron, Mick straightened up to her full height and I still could have stepped on her head. She stretched and said, "Aaron's got some fine writing here. He let me read some last night. Right, Aaron?"

"Yes. I. Did." he answered. I could have sworn he might have been blushing.

"Let me see, Aaron." I put the paper to my eyes and read the lines as Aaron tapped furiously into his keyboard.

"Stop. You. Will. Not—"

But it was too late. I read it anyway. "Okay, F. Scott Fitzgerald. I'm reading the goods."

Chapter One
God is dead like my sister says. He left her with a sucky job working with a bunch of criminals in a prison cell. He left me in my own prison cell, my body. I do not like it that He did this to her and to me. That my dad drinks his paycheck away every month. That our mother went to Florida because she did not want a son in a wheelchair and a daughter who likes making out with girls like Nancy Wilson from Heart.

"Hey, what's this about Nancy Wilson and me kissing?"

Aaron typed. "I. Thought. You. Would. Like. That." He laughed.

Mick said, "God is not dead, Aaron. He's alive and well and—"

"Aaron got it right, don't you think, Margie?" I put his papers back in his mobile home.

Margie cut her eyes at Mick and then looked at me. "Holy Jesus coming off the cross for some time with his peops. Everyone shut up so we can use the wood!"

Mick sidled up to Aaron. "Whatever!" Then she wiped some drool off his face.

I crossed my eyes at Margie. "Okay, tonight at the Mystic," I confirmed. "I'm in the office most of the day today getting ready for the court proceedings next week."

We all bantered with each other for a few more minutes. It was so good to see Margie, and Mick was a walking conundrum but I thought I liked her. She was sweet to Aaron and he could use the attention for sure. Since the court case for the Martinez girl was underway, Emma had canceled several of his writing classes because she was trying to prepare for the trial. So, a new girl for Aaron to ogle was okay by me. Emma had become a monk and two days after the funeral Evan had moved to the south end of town near the rodeo grounds—not far from the Martinez household.

The school year was almost over and the court proceedings for *Martinez vs. Teton County School District* were about to be underway. Oneida and I had interviewed the players; however, Sheriff Williams himself had interviewed Coach Palonski and the principal and Mary Louise's teachers from the high school. The most fraught interview was Susie Clarkson since she was a member of the Jackson police but actually worked for the school system. Judd and Frank interviewed her for two hours, from what I heard, and she was both surly and smug the entire time. She said that Mary Louise Martinez only talked to her about basketball and softball and the Seattle Storm. Yes, she had been to see her in her resource office, but only to talk jump shots, defensive strategies and other players on opposing teams. Susie herself was a Teton High School graduate and had played under Palonski as well. Oneida told me this because Frank had told her.

The Human Rights Campaign and Lambda Legal Defense were following the proceedings and I had to talk to a spokesperson from both organizations every now and again to give them updates. The case was all over the blogosphere. The whole gay world was watching and listening.

If God was dead, as Aaron had written and as I believed, then what was this life worth living for anyway? Suddenly, I was reminded of a time in my youth that I'd long forgotten. A couch, a knife and nothingness. Then a specter appeared, an old dream of being lost on Starling Road and then crying in my mom's arms for hours.

In the months since Mary Louise Martinez's death, I had seen Emma at the Mystic with her mother. We'd exchanged pleasantries, but her quiet demeanor discouraged anything further. Twice she'd stopped to talk with me but mainly she kept to herself. The sexual wash I'd experienced for her was pushed down as far as I could push it because gay girls with any ounce of sense never messed with straight girls. The strange thing was that every time I saw her, her large blue eyes seemed to linger on me in a question, a stare, a something I could never figure out. It actually had all been there since she was a small girl and all the while when she was growing up. Emma Jacobs was an enigma and how she could have endured that Evan cowboy jerk was beyond me. But, then again, how most women put up with male jerkdom was beyond me.

Still, I could feel her presence, and I swallowed my own vibrational energy or whatever it was and let it become a boil on my ass in my hall of fame for women. I could catch a few but never keep any of them. Emma was completely out of reach yet sometimes she crossed my mind at lonely hours of the night when I was idly thinking about unplugging the toaster, or Aaron's medicine refills, or Mary Louise hanging from a basketball hoop. I'd gone to see Emma at her house, candles lit, and papers spread on her coffee table: cup of warm tea by her pen and wearing a V-neck T-shirt and bunny pajama bottoms. I'd found myself standing there in front of her in my own T-shirt and pajama bottoms asking her if she needed a refill or a kiss. She'd respond, "Neither."

Oy. Vay. I prattled on about Aaron's motor home and told Margie and Mick to stop by the Jackson Drug for some homemade ice cream. When they did, I'd told them to call me.

Mick squeaked out like a gerbil, "Do you ever shoot your gun?" What a voice.

"Only when I practice at the shooting range several times a year," I said.

"Can I hold it?" she asked.

"No. I can't allow that. It's against regulations." I sipped my juice.

"What do you think will happen in court?" Margie asked and then sat at the chair by the kitchen table.

I straightened out Aaron's hat and said, "I don't know. Emma is wicked smart but it's the school district they are going up against."

"Yeah, but wasn't the coach having an affair with the girl?" Mick asked. "Do you think the coach and the girl were being sexual?"

"I can't really discuss the details of the case," I said stoically. "You guys be careful with Aaron." I kissed him on the forehead and he smiled, giving me his okay signal.

"We're going to have a blast today," Mick squeaked. "Aaron's letting me ride on his lap all the way to town."

I looked at Aaron. "I'm jealous, Stephen Hawking. I thought I was the only one allowed."

Aaron typed into his keyboard. "Blair. You. Are. The. Princess. Of. All. Deputies. Go. Fight. Those. Assholes."

We laughed and I kissed him on the head again. "You're stupid."

He threw his head back and laughed.

After I got to the courthouse offices, I sat at my own desk near the front of the room, near Oneida's desk. I listened to the birds chirping and singing like a cha-cheering outside of my window. For a minute I listened intently, and then opened up some of the interview papers on the Martinez case. My eyes fell on the testimony of two of the girls I'd interviewed after the incident. I scanned the notes. Each one stated that the coach had an overt policy on alcohol, drugs, and a covert one on homos. She wanted none of it in her locker room, outside of the locker room, or on the court. One of the players noted that there seemed to be some tension between Mary Louise and Coach Palonski the week before her death but didn't know why. I could get nothing else from either one of them.

The attorney for Jackson County Schools, Virgil Steele, stopped in and asked for some discovery evidence from the attorney for the plaintiffs. He was broad-shouldered and gray everywhere. He wore a straw hat that had smashed his hair down and he peered over at me and smiled. His teeth were yellow and stained from chewing tobacco and his boots were muddied with muck and straw.

Just then my cell rang. It was Margie.

"Blair, come quick. Something's wrong with Aaron!"

I stood up and looked out the window. "What's wrong? What's wrong with him?"

Emma walked in through the front doors and waved at me.

"He's fallen out of his wheelchair, he's unconscious. Jesus Christ, Blair. Hurry to Lovely Road. That's where we are. A block from Starling Drive."

"Did you call nine-one-one?"

"Isn't this the fucking call to nine-one-one?" she yelled.

"I'm on my way. I'm on my way!"

I ran past Emma as fast as I could go holding onto my belt and my weapon. On my radio, I called for emergency services at the firehouse to go to the scene and called for an ambulance. I jumped like a motherfucker and twisted my right ankle to pieces as I launched myself into my Jeep. I could hear Emma from the steps of the courthouse, her voice floating in the air as I began my yell at God.

Throwing on my lights and siren, I pulled out of the parking spot feeling my right ankle swell. When I slammed on the brakes to take a corner around to Broadway, the pain seared through my foot and ankle. I called again on my radio. Frantic and frenetic. I called Margie back on her cell phone.

"Margie!" I yelled.

"What? Jesus Christ!"

"Listen," I said calmly. "Check his breathing. Okay? Check to see if air is coming out?"

She put the phone down and I could hear Mick talking to Aaron in her squeaky voice. "Aaron. Aaron. Wake up. Aaron?"

"He doesn't seem to be. I don't know?" Margie was flabbergasted.

"Emergency services are coming. I'm almost there. Don't move him, Margie. His bones are soft. Don't move him!"

There was a pause. "Blair?"

"Yes. Did you move him?"

"Yes. I did."

"It's okay, Margie. Just don't move him anymore."

"Blair?"

"What?" I cornered a corner and sped up to near fifty in a twenty-five.

"I love you. I don't know why I'm saying that. Oh, God!"

"It's okay, Margie. I love you too." I tossed the phone aside. My ankle was pounding every time I pressed on the accelerator or the brakes.

"Fuck you, God. You son of a bitch. I'll hate you even more if you fuck with him any more than you already have! Do you hear me up there? Kiss my boiled sorry ass. Do something more to me. Not to him. Son of a bitch!"

I did not know my mic was open and that the entire sheriff's department could hear me until Oneida called in. "Blair, your mic is open. I'm on my way."

"Shit!"

A moment later, I was at the scene. Leaving my lights on and my car running, I was the first rescue operation to arrive. Margie and Mick were huddled over my brother as if they were sheltering him from the sun and sky. When the slow motion of my life began to pass before me, I almost vomited as I neared my frail brother. Hearing the blare of the fire truck in the distance, I fell knees first and slid on the gravel and dirt toward my brother, the man in my life who was my life, my only link to knowing that I might be okay in the sea of this disgusting world that flung at me its images of anger, abuse, murder, violence, like walking the incisive edge of doom—it all was to me. But, Aaron had made me feel like I could deal. Deal with anything because he provided me with the contrasting, paradoxical hope.

"Aaron," I whispered into his ear.

I checked his breathing, and then cleared his throat with my finger. I pulled out some snotty goo and then pinched his nose with my hand and placed my lips on his and blew. I looked to see his chest rise. Then I counted. I counted once more.

"Thank God you're here," Mick said.

I grabbed her shirt and spat, "Don't say God to me. Don't say God to me." Then I put my hands and arms in the air and screamed. "Don't say God to me!"

I continued with three more puffs and then Ted and Randy, the fire department paramedics, asked me to step aside.

I was out of breath and Margie put her arms around me. Mick stayed over near Aaron and from up the road I could see Diana and Fannie running toward us. Maya Angelou pawed it at breakneck speed in front of them.

The circus was here.

Aaron's manuscript lay strewn all over the street. Some papers with inky splats were wafting in the whimsy of the wind.

His letter to the world.

Maya licked the top of Aaron's dirty, gravelly head as soon as she got into sniffing distance between Aaron and me and Margie. The air smelled of sweat and dust and the blood from Aaron's arms and face. Diana and Fannie huddled around the chaos.

Fannie scratched her head and belly and peered over at Aaron to get a peek. "What happened to the king of drool?" she said.

Luckily Diana was between us as I tripped over her and my swollen ankle trying to grab Fannie's shirt to take the bitch down once and for all.

Diana shoved herself against me, and Oneida put her arms around me from behind, locking me in her grip. "Get in the ambulance, Blair. Don't mess with Fannie. It's your brother you want to focus on, not getting your panties in a twist over someone whose brain hasn't worked right in forty years," Oneida said and I relaxed a bit.

Diana grabbed Maya by the collar to get her away from Aaron. But, the dog sensed something, like animals always do, and Maya just lay down beside him. Diana released the collar and Maya whined.

The paramedics got Aaron on a gurney in about six minutes

flat, Aaron's head dangling over as if it were held on by one tired tendon.

"Get in the ambulance, Blair," Diana yelled at me then grabbed my hand. Maya tried to jump in the back. One of the paramedics had to shoo her down. Good girl.

From outside I could hear a maelstrom of "shut ups" from Diana to Fannie. Mick and Margie stayed with the lunatic fringe and said they would meet me at the hospital. The only hospital in town.

In the back of the ambulance, I knelt down behind Aaron and looked out the back as Ted shut the door.

Randy worked quickly and started an IV and then put patches all over Aaron's chest and stomach. His small frail body was swallowed by the gurney.

His pulse was weak.

Sweat poured from my temples and ran down the sides of my cheeks. As we pulled away, I saw Emma arriving. Her face was focused on the back of the ambulance and she walked to her mother and aunt. For a split second, I thought she could see me through the dim glass panels of the ambulance. For a split second, I thought she penetrated the doors and was in there with me. For a split second, I must have gone mad.

Once we got to the hospital, Oneida was there within minutes of the gurney being whisked away to an ER room. I was limping through the hallway, Oneida stopped me.

"Come this way," she said and led me down a different corridor.

"Oneida, you flipping weirdo. Can't you see I'm limping here and want to get to my brother?"

"Blair, you have to come with me to get that ankle of yours checked out. It looks like a soccer ball down there. You need to have someone look at it."

Through the double doors of the emergency room, in walked everyone from the original scene: Mick, Margie, Diana and Emma. Fannie was outside smoking a cigarette with Maya Angelou tethered to a pole.

I gestured to Fannie. "Tell her to send smoke signals to all the mystics in the world. Will ya?" I asked Diana. "Tell her the king of drool is drowning in his own fluids and we need the mystics to take a break from their fucking book tours and swinging from the Hima-fucking-layas and eating the juice of the diamond fig that will bring them health, wealth and prosperity. You hear me! Do you?" The snot flew from my nose.

"I'll let her know." Diana came to me and put her hands on my shoulders.

"Diana? Why? What?" I asked, then rubbed my nose on my shirt.

Emma came from behind Mick. "It's okay, Blair. What can we do for you?"

I burst into tears. "You can tell Fannie to fuck off. Then you can do a special Tarot reading that doesn't have the death card. Then you can—I don't know. You tell me."

Margie stepped toward us. "Mick and I will take Fannie off your shoulders, Blair. Here." She reached out her hand. I grabbed it. "Let's go see your brother. Mick, grab that wheelchair."

Mick squeaked and looked bedazzled. "What wheelchair?"

"This one," Emma said as she caught one sitting idly by the hallway near the water fountain. "Sit down, Blair."

I obliged and sat. Mick reached for a pedal and pulled it up so I could put my leg up.

"Where's Aaron Wingfield?" Emma asked a nurse behind the counter.

Margie leaned on the counter. "Wingfield. Aaron? Which room is he in?"

"Down the hall and to the left. He's in with the doctor, I'm not sure how many people can go back there." She looked down at her paper and by the time she looked back up, we were all gone, like true mystics. We floated down the hallway in a still point of time. Emma and Margie pushed me and Diana and Mick rattled along behind. We were a caravan of gypsies from a time long ago.

For a short moment, the fog of my small life lifted.

My past life regression, portentous and ugly, came to me fast and hard. I began to think of the battle between the French and the Maid of Orleans, Joan of Arc, and how in another gender, we all must have done battle with one another. A midget. A gypsy.

A realtor. A sheriff. A teacher. A band of choristers on horses tromping through marshy grasses, drunk on fear and religion, breaking bad to fight off the English to defend our king. Now, we were just women, small, semi-effusive in our dealings with the public at large, trying to find a small crippled man who'd collapsed in the middle of a street in a small town swallowed by big mountains.

We turned a corner and found Aaron. I inhaled deeply and stood up.

"Sit down, Blair!" Diana barked.

I did as she commanded.

Emma wheeled me to his side and his face was nestled small on a pillow. His eyelids looked swollen as if he'd been crying. His keyboard and iPod were on the chair next to him. Emma scooped both up and handed them to Diana. Then, Emma put her hand on my back, a place I'd known before with her, and the warmth of it penetrated to a new core opening up in me, like a miniature bloom.

"Aaron. Aaron? It's me. Blair. Can you hear me?" I leaned over to him and grabbed his bulbous, veiny hand. From behind, I could hear Margie on her cell phone out in the hall talking to someone and Mick paced the floor in cowboy boots that had tiny sparkly spurs on them.

Diana went to the other side of the bed amongst the bleating of the monitors and his IV. "Aaron? We know you like getting attention, but isn't this going a bit too far? If we get a couple of rock stars here to sing to you will that help? Hmm? We need to pray over his body, Emma. Now. Let's pray now."

I could not balk at this. I did not have the energy. Emma and Diana did a methodic Lord's Prayer and then a Hail Mary. I knew the Lord's Prayer but not Mary's. I let the two Catholics handle it. Then I put my hand on Aaron's head—it was warm. I thought about his baseball cap lying in the street and began to cry.

A nurse came in to check his IV and monitor for his heart. "We're running some blood work and the doctor has ordered a CT scan. After that, we'll talk to him about what's next. He's stable but we need to find out what the results say."

Emma put her other hand on my shoulder and squeezed. I put my head on Aaron's shoulder and whispered into his ear. "Yo. Stephen. Hawking. What are you doing?"

Then, out of the blue, Dad walked in.

He took off his cowboy hat and tripped over a cord and came to settle next to Diana. He scratched his beard and I looked up at him.

"I think he's had another stroke, Dad."

"Yeah. Yeah. Seems like it. I heard you helped him get here." He looked to Diana then to Emma. My heart swooned for the both of them.

"She put her mouth on his mouth and blew like a banshee," Mick squeaked out and then turned to Margie who was still on the phone. Margie shrugged and pointed to Diana and Mick to follow her out, leaving Emma and me and Dad alone with Aaron.

Emma broke in after a long silence. "Blair. Do you want to be alone?"

I thought about it for a second. "No, you can stay." She released her warm hands from me and stepped back some. "Dad, do you think we should call Mom?" I asked.

He shuffled his feet and looked at Emma and then at me. "How's the Martinez family doing?"

Emma looked puzzled but then said, "Fine. As best as one can expect after losing a daughter in that way."

"Dad?" I questioned.

"Let me think it over. She might just get in the way. But, I'll handle it." He regarded his son. "Poor little Aaron. He's gotten the short end of the stick once again."

"He never even got up to bat, Dad."

Emma sensed some tension. "He's a very good writer, Mr. Wingfield."

"That right?" Dad leaned against the hospital curtain then staggered a bit. "What does he write about?"

"Well, he writes about what he knows. I guess he can tell you the rest when he wakes up." She paused. "Blair, you okay with your pain?"

I paused wondering what she meant then said, "The ankle?

Oh, the ankle is nothing compared to this. Nothing. I'll be sore for a while. I know you're working like a mule on that case of yours. You can go Emma."

"I'll stay. If that's okay with you and Mr. Wingfield," she said.

"David. Call me David." Dad pulled up a chair.

Margie and Mick and Diana and the rest of the troupe left the hospital and went back to the Mystic to get some supplies for me and for Aaron. By the time they got back to us, Aaron had been moved to ICU and Dad and Emma and I were in his room drinking coffee and saying very little. Dad spiked his with his silver dollar flask to maintain his quiet affect. Mick put Aaron's iPod on the table with speakers. When she turned it on, it blasted out "Barracuda" by Heart. She jerked it toward her and turned the volume down and played a ballad by them instead. Mick was trying hard and I started to like the midget. Diana came in wearing a long black leather coat and she went directly to Aaron and kissed him on the head and then let her hand remain on it for quite a while. Margie sat next to me and put her hand on my thigh. I told her not to become a lesbian too soon and then she squeezed it really hard till I laughed.

The doctor confirmed what we'd all thought. He reported that Aaron's CT scan showed he'd had a stroke and that we'd have to see if he improved overnight with the IV and all the good vibes he was getting from his vigil. I almost flipped him off but Emma grabbed my hand before I could do it. Mick sneered at him and Dad left with the doctor to go to the liquor store.

Mick and Diana went home several hours later. Margie stretched out on a cot they brought in and we all did a quiz from one of Oprah's magazines on relationships. I rotated ice off and on my ankle and Emma went off to fetch me dinner, late.

"I think I'm getting some vibe-age from the Emma-meister over to you, Ms. Panty-twisted," Margie told me. Her black cowboy boots were scuffed from the accident, and her sweater revealed some cleavage. Her black, silky hair was in a clip and tendrils outlined each ear.

"What?" I asked and then brushed Aaron's hair off his forehead.

"Dudette, she's been sitting next to you all day and bringing you coffee and hasn't barely done or said anything except when it related to you."

"She's years younger than I am and s, t, r, a, i, g, h, t."

"Emma Jacobs is a big fat lesbo, Blair. She's been looking at you like you were a goddess on a horse ever since she was a kid. Every time we've been around, she's looked at you with those enormous oceanic blue eyes and I think she practically has to change her panties."

"Margie, for God's sake, I've got a sick brother here and we don't need to be talking panties."

"Since when did you get to be so pretentious and uptight?" Margie put the magazine down and opened up a lipstick case.

I leaned back in my chair. "I don't know. I don't think Emma is a big fat lesbian. She just broke up with her boyfriend not long ago. They were together for quite awhile. Besides, I'm not bringing a virgin lesbian over to my side of the fence. It feels too weird. I've known Emma since she was a kid."

Margie sat up. "Blair, the problem with you is that you have no faith, you agnostic atheist asshole. And, dumbass, you just gave away how you feel."

"What do you mean?" I suddenly got very tired.

The door opened as Margie all but yelled, "You have feelings for Emma Jacobs. Just freaking admit it will you? I can..." Emma walked in carrying a tray, "...feel it." Margie finished her thought, then laughed to try and cover it up but there was no doubt, Emma had heard.

Quietly and with wide eyes, Emma brought me a tray from the cafeteria that had three sandwiches on it. She handed one to Margie, who smiled at her. She handed one to me and I nodded a thank you. And then, she took the last one for herself.

For about five minutes, we all ate in semistrained silence. I glanced at Margie. She glanced at me. I glanced at Aaron. I glanced back at Margie who nodded her California head over to Emma. Finally, my eyes fell on Emma.

Finally, my eyes fell for Emma. When she cut her eyes to me quickly and boldly, I knew. She knew.

I quivered.

When Emma went home an hour later, Margie wrapped up the remnants of her sandwich and tossed it in the wastepaper basket like she was playing for the Lakers. "See, Deputy Dildo Fife?"

See, I did.

CHAPTER NINE

He lay in a coma.

Diana and Fannie and Emma set up a prayer line for Aaron. Emma said that it was the world's greatest wireless connection—she'd seen it on a T-shirt once at Yale. *Whatever*, I thought.

The following week, the court proceedings in *Martinez vs. Teton County School District* began its carnival epic rodeo-esque masquerade ball down the center of town to the courthouse two blocks past Broadway and town square on good ole boy Cottage Avenue. It arrived as a civil case involving wrongful death and bullying. We all agreed that the biggest dumbass on the hotseat was the coach. The case was a no-brainer. Margie had told us all that. Martinez and the coach were having an affair. The coach, as we all had known, had been a closet lesbian since the sixth century B.C. and the husband and two kids had been her defense to the heterosexual world that you could be heterosexual and still look like a big fat dyke. Plus, the resource cop was a closeted dyke who should have known better. Margie said that the Martinez family was in good hands with Emma as their attorney although the big fat defense attorney would rip her a new asshole but that I could assuage her soul by making out with her behind the barn at the Mystic Market.

"Shut up, Margie!" I buttoned my brown sheriff's shirt.

Margie came into my bedroom as I attached my name tag. "Do you know who you are by attaching your name tag? Do you point to people and say, 'I'm Deputy Blair Wingfield'? Do you need a bullet for your pocket?"

Mick laughed from Aaron's desk as she noodled over some stuff online about the court case. I was headed to the courthouse to do security with Oneida.

"I thought you guys would be headed out of town by now and on your way back to California to drive the Pacific Coast Highway, smoke hookahs and listen to garage band rock while you sell real estate and take on the newest hippie chick band full of tattoos, tits and glittered toenails."

"Yo." Margie put her hands in the air. "Stop with the alliteration, Deputy. You might think we think you might be smart."

Mick turned around with her smallness and her shrill voice re-echoed through my bungalow. "The case is all over the Internet. Looks like we're staying for a bit…perhaps through the end of the trial. There are a few local people we're going to see and then we're headed off to L.A. for a CD release gig for one of my up-and-coming female bands—Lost Princess."

Margie handed me my belt and reminisced. "It's so cool to see you dress up. Remember when we used to go into the outbuilding behind the Mystic Market and play dress up as kids? You were always the pirate and I was the Queen of England. You were extra cute in the eye patch, Blair."

I wiped some dust from my bureau mirror. "Margie, you looked like a Barbie doll all dressed up and then we drank from those teacups and planned revenge on the American alliance that had formed against us."

Margie fingered my belt and I swatted her away.

Margie re-clipped her hair. "Then we would go out and have our own sword fight by Cache Creek and you always, always let me win. Why?"

"Good swashbucklers always let the girl win," I said then grabbed the belt and put it on and ran my hands through my damp hair. "Will you swashbuckler to the hospital for a few hours while I'm at work?"

Fannie rapped at my door and came in unannounced. "Blair? Blair?" She looked at me wide-eyed and with a question. Mick stood up and spurred herself over to see what she was holding in her hand.

"Fannie Crabwell, you better have a good reason for barging in on my women's fest here." I grabbed a cup of coffee from the counter and eyed Margie who marched toward Fannie as an age-old queen might do.

Margie leaned into to her. "Fannie." She wrangled her hand into hers while Fannie just stared at me. "Come with me back to the Market. We'll get some of those homemade biscuits dirty Diana makes, eh?"

Fannie jerked free then held up a bound leather folio that held loose papers between the bindings. "It's Aaron's, Blair. I went back to the street and got it. You have to read this. Please. The wheelchair wanker has something to say."

I blew coffee out of my mouth and into the sink.

"Out. Out, Fannie before I become part of the kind of crime that Jackson Hole, Wyoming has never seen."

"Oh my!" Mick drew her hands to her heart. "Margie, you better get her out of here before we have a postal situation."

Fannie moved closer to me. "He talks about you, Blair. You." Fannie smiled at me and a hush fell over us. "It's not half bad. Who are you?" Her crooked teeth were yellow crags and her forehead was a pinched loaf but for a second, I tried to listen.

"I'm Blair Ignatius Underwear, straight from the Confederacy of Dunces. You?" I adjusted my ball cap. "I'm going to the courthouse. Margie, will you text me from the hospital in case something changes. I'll be over to sit with the wheelchair wanker after my shift is over."

Margie came over to my side and grabbed my mug from me. "Go, Blair. We can handle Fannie Crabwell. Go. Go to court. Emma will be glad for it."

Fannie looked at me with the weirdest expression, then from her pocket pulled her stack of dirtied Tarot cards and began to shuffle them. Her expression turned from grim to the grim reaper. "It's you, Blair. All along I thought it was Emma. But it's you." Fannie's eyes darted from Mick to Margie and we all glanced at each other and then shrugged.

Finally, I said, "Do you think, Fannie, if we pray to Shatki Gawain or to Deepak Chopra or the popular black psychic, who's that, Latoya Jackson? They'd show up and give us the power to heal Aaron?"

"How can you not like someone in a wheelchair?" Mick asked Fannie. A question we'd all thought but had never undertaken to issue from our lips.

Fannie stood back like she was frightened by three women staring at her. Her butt hit the screen door and it cracked itself open allowing a small breeze to move through the kitchen. Through Aaron's window by his bed, I saw a red hawk land in the patchy grass. Two chipmunks scampered away. When my gaze returned to Fannie, her face was lit up like a Christmas tree.

"Aaron's a good man. He's going to die, but he's a good man."

On the word "die," no one, not even Margie could have stopped me. I went straight for Fannie, straight for her throat. I put both hands on her neck and she dropped the manuscript she'd bound and grappled against me as we tossed ourselves onto the front porch and hit the dirt. I found myself lying on top of the mother of the woman I was falling in love with. The contradiction and terrible fear penetrated me suddenly and as Margie and Mick came from behind, I'd already released my chokehold on her and removed myself.

Fannie rolled away from me and slowly got to her feet. Grass was sticking from her red hair and her pinched lips became more severe as she put her hands on her hips. "Well, Blair. I guess your wheelchair wanker of a brother has one thing over on you."

"Yeah, Fannie, what's that?" I asked, breathing hard.

"He'd have to run me over with his wheelchair." And with that, she went into a laughing hysteria none of us expected. "Run me over with his wheelchair. Yep." Then she tore into some more laughter.

Mick put her hand down to help me up. "You should have been a sail. You fly like the wind, Blair."

"Thanks, Mick. I got it from that." I pointed to the broom sitting sadly at the edge of the porch.

Margie laughed. "You ride the broom and Fannie here rides bullshit. How long you been riding the bullshit, Fannie?"

Fannie cackled again. "For more years than you know. Hell, for more years than I know. Emma knows though. She always knows."

On that note, I left the Hatfield and Mick-oys and went to work. Once at the courthouse and amongst the people from the left and people from the right, I felt safe again. Lost and safe in a sea of people where no one could see Blair. Just the name tag and the uniform and the gun belt.

I heard a TV reporter say that emotions were running high. At the corner of Cottage Avenue and Wythe Street, I saw Ray with his bag of whiskey. As we both made eye contact, I nodded at him.

My pants felt looser than normal. A week at the hospital had left me eating even more protein bars and drinking coffee Diana brought me in a thermos from the Mystic Market.

Aaron was in a coma caused by a blood clot to the brain. At least it wasn't hemorrhaging and we were waiting for him to come out of his "sleepy state" as Mick put it. She played music for him and she and Margie sat with him while I put in a few shifts for the biggest case Jackson had seen in a long time.

By count on the way up the steps, I could see three, maybe four news trucks parked out front with camera and sound men and women and commentators and journalists all milling about looking for someone to harass. I thought they should all go to the Mystic and harass Fannie, but her acting out was now a different weird. She almost seemed sane.

My interest in the manuscript she'd bound for Aaron was

high and I wondered if his words about me were true or surreal. Right now, everything was surreal except for the edifice and the concrete beneath my leather shoes. Every turn of my body seemed to feel for Aaron, every turn of my mind seemed to feel for Emma.

As I entered the courtroom, I saw Oneida and nodded toward her. I glanced at the clock, the flags on both sides of the judge's bench, the chamber. Like a church but without the crosses and the white wafers and the white collars. Here the robe was different and Judge Joe Archer was back in his own inner chambers, I imagined, fixing his robe and slicking back his hair. The bailiff was Robert Perrins, a husky young deputy on the force. I nodded to him as I went forward in the court and to a stand near the judge's bench. I was the only officer who was there for extra security reasons, so I took a seat on the right side of the court. I vacillated between judge and jury, depending on the need.

Emma strode in a few minutes later with Mr. and Mrs. Martinez. Both looked the same as they'd looked the day of the funeral: drawn tight, stress in their respective faces, darkness swallowing their eyes in a futile sadness, and their bodies looked hunched. Mr. Martinez needed some translation as his English was broken and Mrs. Martinez helped him as they took their seats on the right side of the court where a large desk and several chairs waited for them.

About ten seconds after their arrival, the defense attorney and the superintendent of Teton County Schools as well as the principal arrived to take their seats in at the same layout on the opposite side. Each wore dark suits and cowboy boots. Coach Palonski came in with her husband, and a few of the students from Teton High ambled in, in jeans and loose shirts and carefully crafted cool haircuts. Some sat on the right, some on the left. The courtroom shenanigans went on for a few minutes and then the court was opened to the general public. I saw Diana come in and sit in the back. She'd left the Mystic to Fannie and Tyler, the bartender and day cook, to run.

The courtroom became quiet enough to hear a pin drop as the twelve jurors entered and sat in the pews to the left of the judge's high desk. I recognized the bartender from the Cowboy Bar and several ranchers from the barn where Evan was a farrier. Of the twelve three were women, two of whom I recognized from the old bridge club where my mom had played for years. There was one Hispanic in the lot and no blacks. Then, I saw her: Carleen Proust. Real estate agent to Evan and a missed arrest by me. She saw me and winked. A jury trial had been requested by the Martinez family and Emma to determine the guilt and assess the appropriate damages if they won the civil case.

The bailiff came in and announced, "All rise." Everyone stood as Judge Archer came to the bench and knocked his knocker for everything to come to order. In my head, I floated once again to Mary Louise—wondering how it could come to this for such a young life. How she felt there was no way out. I wondered if Aaron ever felt the same way, trapped in his body, trapped in his mind to spend life over and over again like someone on a Ferris wheel but without the people and fun.

Then there was a hand on my shoulder. I thought of Emma, but when I turned, it was Oneida. She motioned for me to come with her to the back of the courtroom.

"CNN just arrived." She looked around.

"So?"

"So, are you smoking crack or just TV-less? CNN is the biggest news thing on TV."

"Tell me. Are they as big as what's happened to my brother or the Martinez family?"

"Blair, you aren't getting the point."

"No, 'Neida. You aren't. I don't care if Barbara Walters is out there. Or Oprah for that matter."

"What's gotten into you?"

Emma started to speak and I turned to listen.

"Your honor, and ladies and gentlemen of the jury, this proceeding is to determine who is at fault in the death of Ms. Mary Louise Martinez, who on March twenty-sixth of this year committed suicide by hanging at the Teton High School gymnasium." Standing at her desk, she flipped through a legal pad and leaned on the table. She shifted to one side and I looked at her backside, the crook of her elbow, the hair half inside her white collar, the sway and curve of her hip against the fabric of her blue-black dress. Her slender hands knuckled to the table. Her long porcelain legs, like ballerina's legs, stuck inside the dark leather of small pumps.

My heart beat. One. Two. Three.

"Blair?" Oneida woke me up.

"Nothing. There's nothing we can do about CNN. If it attracts more people, then we'll call on the department in Rock Springs to come and help with crowd control. Okay?"

"Your ankle feeling okay?" she whispered.

"Yeah, it's just my Achilles tendon that's sore mainly. I banged it up nicely last week."

"Aaron okay?"

"Still in a coma..."

There was an "Ahem" from the judge as he waved us up. Oneida and I came up and took our posts.

Emma Jacobs was ready to flap some words.

CHAPTER TEN

Every inch of the courtroom reeked of silent insanity. The tiny wispy scratching of handbags and shuffling of papers made it echo like an ocean shell. Courtroom attendees ogled each other and the deputies. The courtroom reporter's fingers were poised over her machine and the walls seemed to close in around the bustle of trying to be quiet, to settle the nerves. I could smell the June dirt of cows and horses in the air from the shoes and boots. The energy reverberated and everyone knocked around and fumbled and bumbled trying their best not to get up and holler something really loudly. Anything. Even I did.

Emma went on to present the Martinez side of the case. She read from her notes and then added extemporaneously. "Your honor, between noon and one o'clock p.m. on March twenty-sixth, Mary Louise Martinez, an eighteen-year-old senior at

Teton High School, hanged herself in the school gymnasium. She hanged herself after an off-season intramural practice and weightlifting session. She hanged herself after what the court will find was a bullying campaign launched against her by, your honor, some of the teammates themselves and the coach. For the record, the coach of Teton High School is Mildred Alice Palonski. In addition, the school's resource officer, a Ms. Susan Jean Clarkson, is named in the suit as testimony will find that she was informed by Mary Louise Martinez of these bullying incidents but did nothing to stop them. Neither did any of her teachers. In this country students have a right to be included in sports and after-school activities. Title Nine says, and I quote, *No person in the United States shall, on the basis of sex, be excluded from participation in, be denied the benefits of, or be subjected to discrimination under any educational program or activity receiving Federal financial assistance.*

"Title Nine, Your Honor, provides a very charged statement here and that is, 'no person—no person—shall be subject to discrimination under any educational program.'" She flipped a page of her legal pad over and went on. "Just this school year, anti-bullying measures added sexual orientation to the student code of conduct. A GSA, that is a Gay-Straight Alliance, was formed as well. Yet, even though these footholds were in place to engender equality to LGBT students, the covert bullying by a sign that says 'no alcohol, no drugs, and no lesbians,' rings as awful today as it did for the Penn State basketball players over twenty or so years ago. The plaintiffs are seeking compensatory damages in this case because Mary Louise Martinez spoke out again and again. But, no one listened. As this trial unfolds, I believe that you, ladies and gentlemen of the jury, will find that there is no doubt that this is a death that should have never happened, a case should have never made it to this courtroom, a kind of bullying based on sexual orientation that should never, ever continue here or anywhere. Thank you."

Both judge and jury remained impassive in facial expression each listened intently to her statements and then awaited for Virgil Steele to lay his claim to the land of the case.

"Your honor, ladies and gentlemen of the jury, on behalf of

the Teton County Schools, we reject the statements that have been made concerning the death of Ms. Mary Louise Martinez. It is our position, that while tragic indeed, this was a suicide by a young girl—a troubled young girl—who happened to perform this act on school property. Teton High School is in no way liable for the actions of this troubled youth and we seek to have the civil suit dismissed. It is our opinion that this suicide is a private matter. One that should have been resolved by the parents of the student."

After these brief opening statements from opposing attorneys, Alicia Stone was called to the stand and brought in from the witness sequestering room. She was the first player I interviewed in March. After taking the oath and stating her name, she answered Emma's preliminary question that she was a student and basketball player at Teton High School. In her dark flared slacks and V-neck sweater that had an angel pinned to the collar, she uncomfortably swiveled in her seat as Emma prepared to continue asking questions. I checked my phone for any silent texts on Aaron and then watched carefully. Emma glanced at me, momentarily. I nodded. Yes. You. Can. I felt like a political bumper sticker but I liked this girl.

Visibly nervous, Alicia Stone took to checking the jury, her mother in the back, and her nails.

"Alicia. May I call you Alicia?" Emma asked. She moved to the right and to the left of the courtroom like a stealthy cat, sleek and calculating. My internal smile-o-meter sang a song for her. Good question. Get that name right. I looked at Oneida and she nodded at me.

Alicia twiddled a loose strand of her blond hair from a ponytail. "Yes, ma'am."

"We have testimony here that you were a good friend to Mary Louise Martinez."

"Objection." Virgil Steele slowly stood up. "Your Honor, we kindly object to the usage of the phrase 'friend' and want to establish the meaning. Does counsel mean friend or more than a friend?"

Emma noticeably reacted to this dim-witted objection. She clasped the back of her neck with her hands. Almost involuntarily, I adjusted my tie and looked down my nose at Steele in disdain.

"Overruled." Judge Archer waved Virgil off and nodded for Emma to move on. Bored with his life, the case, or the surreal feel of the courtroom, he closed his eyes to listen to Emma.

Emma went directly at Steele's objection. "Alicia were you friends or were you more than that, like boyfriend and girlfriend?"

Into the small mic, Alicia continued to twiddle her hair, leaned forward and said, "Just friends. That's it."

"Thank you. Now, can you tell us a little about Mary Louise and your friendship and the activities you were involved in."

Alicia looked at her mom. Judge Archer still had his eyes closed and Virgil Steele leaned back in his chair, his arms behind his head. Evidently, he was comatose too. "We've been friends since middle school when we played basketball together. She was a shooting guard and I was a number four forward. Her mom is friends with my mom."

Mrs. Martinez smiled gently and Mr. Martinez scribbled on a piece of paper. Oneida walked to the side of the courtroom toward the bailiff to see who the next witness was, I guessed. We would rotate in and out to retrieve them.

"Good," Emma said then sauntered toward the jury. All eyes were on the young, hot attorney—taking on the bullies of the world.

"Now, Alicia. Can you tell me and the court here about your basketball team?"

"Well, we're pretty good. We won states year before last and this year we lost to Laramie in the regionals. Three points. Lost it at the foul line."

"Okay, now tell me about the month after regionals. I assume you lost in February, is that correct?"

"Yes."

"And, by early to mid-March, you were back in the gym doing what?"

"Well, Coach likes us to work year-round. So, we were doing weights and light intramural games with other girls from the school."

"For the record, Alicia, will you name the coach?"

"That's Coach Palonski. Millie Palonski." Alicia sat back, seemingly relieved.

Emma walked closer to Alicia. "Can you tell us more about Coach Palonski's relationship with Mary Louise Martinez?"

"Objection." Virgil placed his hands on the table and stood up and leaned over his belly. "This case is not about the coach of the team but about the nature of the girl's mind."

"Virgil, sit down. I'll allow it. Go ahead, Ms. Jacobs." He closed his eyes again.

Everyone in the courtroom stilled and Alicia said, "Well, they were close. Sometimes Coach Palonski has some of the players over to her house on Sundays to watch football."

"The whole team?" Emma asked.

"No, just ones she asked in her office every now and then."

"And were you one of those players?"

"Yes."

"Tell me, Alicia. Did Coach Palonski have any unwritten or written rules regarding players' behaviors on or off the court?"

"Yes."

"What were they?"

Alicia looked at her mother. "Well, it's always been a known fact about the program. No alcohol. No drugs. And, no lesbians."

"Thank you, Alicia. I have no further questions."

Virgil stood up and moved toward Alicia adjusting his belt much like the way Sheriff Williams shifted his. "Alicia, can you tell me this. Did Coach Palonski ever sit the entire team down and say those very words, 'no alcohol, no lesbians, no drugs?'"

"No, sir. It was just a known fact."

"Yes, but stick with the answer. She never sat you or your teammates down and said out loud and proud that you could not drink, nor do drugs, nor be a lesbian?" He hammered this question out, his voice rising.

"No." Alicia moved nervously.

"Let me ask you this, Alicia. It's good not to drink, right?"

"Yes."

"It's good not to do drugs, right."

"Yes."

"In your mind, it's good not to be a lesbian, right?"

"Objection." Emma stood up, pursed and austere. "Your Honor, this line of questioning is leading to a moral question and does not directly nor properly address the case at hand."

Archer opened his left eye. "I'll allow it."

Alicia looked at her nails and bit her pinky.

Virgil asked again. "It's not, in your honest opinion, good or right to be a lesbian, is it?"

"No."

"How many other players on the team would agree with you, Alicia?"

"Most all, I guess."

"Objection." Emma stood again. "Your Honor, I would presume we all know that Alicia here cannot give us the feelings of all of the basketball players at Teton High."

"Sustained. Mr. Steele, what else do you have?"

"Alicia, did you notice anything different in the weeks or the days before Mary Louise Martinez took her own life?"

Alicia paused. "The only thing any of us noticed is that she started eating lunch by herself and she wasn't talking much. But, then again, she never really said much. She just focused on her schoolwork and playing ball."

"That's all, Your Honor."

Emma called her next witness: Susie Clarkson. I did another internal vomit. I was mortified I'd slept with her.

Wearing a simple navy pantsuit, Susie entered and took her oath. The Martinez family had a squadron of players behind Emma in the courtroom and everyone watched the chunky butch, with her thick neck and sandy blond hair combed to the side, stride to the stand and sit down.

Emma approached and asked Susie to state her full name and address and employer.

Susie leaned into the microphone. "My name is Susan Jean Clarkson. I live at 8714 Wytheland Road. I am employed by both the Jackson police force and Teton County Schools as the school's resource officer."

"Thank you. Now, Ms. Clarkson. Did you know Mary Louise Martinez?"

"Of course, everyone knew Mary Louise. She was a great basketball player."

"Is it correct that Mary Louise Martinez came to you on more than one occasion to talk to you about the signs in the locker room?"

"No. Mary Louise came by my office but she never talked about anything but sports and food. She loved tacos." Susie looked at the jury and gave a slight smile.

"Ms. Clarkson, you are under oath. Do you deny that she ever showed you a sign from the locker room?"

She squirmed. The courtroom squirmed. Judge Archer opened one eye to peek.

"Yes. I mean, no," Susie stated.

"No what?"

Virgil stood up. "Objection, Your Honor. She's trying to confuse the witness." He hiked his pants up.

Judge Archer opened the other eye.

"Let me repeat the question, Your Honor. Ms. Clarkson, did Mary Louise Martinez talk to you about the signs in the locker room?"

Susie paused. "She did not come out overtly and talk about them. She just handed one to me once. Last year. She didn't say anything about it. She just gave it to me and that was all."

"What did you do after she gave you the sign?"

"I put it in my drawer and decided to think about it. Then, frankly, I forgot about it. It was near Christmas last year and since I stuck it in the drawer. Yeah, I sort of forgot about it."

"You forgot about it?" Emma's voice held polite incredulity.

"Yes. I had several drug issues that week and completely forgot about it. Honestly."

"You forgot about it? Correct?"

"Correct."

"Forgot about it. Thank you, Ms. Clarkson. That's all. That's enough."

Virgil Steele rose but Judge Archer said, "Watch it, counsel."

"Sorry, Your Honor."

Steele placed his hand on the back of the square-faced

superintendent of Teton schools sitting next to him. He paused and whispered something to the principal.

He approached the stand. "Ms. Clarkson. How long have you been a resource officer at Teton High School?"

"Going on seven years," she said, looking at him warily.

"And, in that seven years, could you characterize the kind of support you've given to the students and faculty."

She relaxed at this friendly approach. "Sure. I coordinate all of the emergency evacuation procedures of the school in case of catastrophic incident. I handle all of the discipline matters involving students and the law—mainly truancy, drugs and fights. I also train all of the faculty on bullying and how to stop and prevent it from happening…"

"Stop there. Does this include sexual orientation?"

"Yes. This year, we've included it into our training."

"Thank you. That's all, Your Honor."

"Ms. Jacobs, redirect?"

"No, Your Honor. But we'd like to reserve the right to recall the witness later if necessary."

"Very well. Let's recess for a twenty-minute break." Two witnesses in and the judge was tired. Or needed to take a leak.

When court resumed, Virgil and Emma were standing at the judge's large desk in deep discussion. I watched the jurors come back in and Carleen Proust eyed me one more time. I momentarily caught her eye, then looked at Mrs. Martinez who, for some odd reason, was also looking my way. I made an attempt to smile at her and she smiled back at me. She whispered into her husband's ear, something in Spanish, I surmised, and then he looked my way. She then motioned me over. Since the gavel had not gone down, I stepped toward her.

Mrs. Martinez put her hand on my back and I leaned in to see what was on the desk in front of her. A cross, a rosary and a picture of Mary Louise playing basketball.

In a thick Spanish accent, she spoke. "You're de officer who, eh, escorted us around town when we, eh, put Mary Louise to the cemetery? I seen you in town with your brother Aaron. He sick?"

"Yes, ma'am," I said.

"Me and Grandy here. We pray for him. For you."

The gavel went down. So did my heart.

CHAPTER ELEVEN

After court was over for the day and the flimflam back and forth between Emma and Virgil over three additional witnesses, the story remained the same. No one was really giving up much information and everyone had a reason for not seeing the blinking neon signs of bigotry and bullying. *I put it in the drawer and forgot it.* She put her own lesbianism in a drawer and forgot about it...dumb Log Cabin Republican. Sometimes gay people were our own worst enemies. Clarkson was evidence to that. Gay people who voted for George Bush were an insult to the LGBT people and our plight. They might as well be straight—I don't want them on my team.

I went to the Mystic to get something to eat before heading to the hospital. Once there, I felt warmth pervade me that I had not felt in a long while. The tense yet frenetic courtroom was unbearable, the sterile smelling hospital unbearable, but more so was my empty bungalow without Stephen Hawking to push around.

Diana brought me a plate of scrambled eggs, bacon, biscuits and a stack of three pancakes. She set down a cup of coffee, iced tea, orange juice and a side car of cranberry juice. We laughed.

"Eat. You're losing too much weight." Diana returned to her usual post and sat down and put on her reading glasses to do bills. Diana—my mom when there was no mom.

"Yeah, eat," Emma said as she sat down next to me. She had changed from her lawyer duds into jeans and a jacket.

"Hey, you big lawyer, you. Shouldn't you be home studying big words like plaintiff and pontificate and Pope?"

"Pope? That's not so hard, Blair." She smiled at me and took a piece of bacon from my plate.

"Don't flirt with me, Emma. I'm too tired and too confused by my life anyway."

Two fishermen entered the Mystic to buy some tackle and Tyler took them down the aisle to find some lures.

"Come with me for a while after you eat your lumberjack dinner?"

"If 'come with me' means going to see Aaron, then yes. I need to get to the hospital." I snatched my bacon back and shoveled it into my mouth.

"Blair. Have I ever asked you to do anything in my whole life? I need a break for a few hours. Mick and Margie can handle watching over Aaron. I want to show you something important."

"This sounds so romantic, Emma. Is it your house? Because I've already been there." I forked some pancake in my mouth and smiled.

"Go with her, dummy," Fannie said from the back.

I stuck my tongue out at Fannie and she laughed and closed the curtain. A Tarot prospector walked in just after her.

I relinquished control over the mystical witches.

Once in Emma's car, I stopped complaining and just let her drive. She had said that sometimes you just need to get away and take a break. That applied to me too.

"I noticed you looked tired in court today, Blair," she said. "You've got too much on you with Aaron and working…"

"You're doing a good job, Emma. Plus you look pretty cute in that lawyerly outfit of yours. When did you find your voice? You were always such a quiet kid." I rolled the window down and let the wind hit my face and hair.

"I found it halfway between my mother, Yale and Evan."

She said it so perfunctorily that I almost laughed but restrained myself.

We went east down Broadway, did a loop around the rodeo grounds, and then landed in front of Snow King Mountain. The mountain I'd skied on in high school. It was steep and majestic and had two slopes that formed a very feminine-shaped bare spot on two sides of the mountain. A few summer tourists were milling about and the ski lift operated all year because of the restaurant at the top that overlooked the Gros Ventre mountains that themselves created another valley between them.

"Emma, you wanted to show me this?" I asked incredulously. "I've seen it ten million times."

I got out of the car and went around to the front fender and peered up the brazen fields of green that rose in a steepness that felt like one might catapult off if one were not careful. The mountain said, *"Come, climb me if you can. Ski me if you can."* The slope was daring and I always had a tiny bit of reverence for its awesome prodigiousness and the feel it gave me about the people who like ants climbed and sputtered all over it.

"You haven't been here with me. So, let's take the ski lift and get to the top. What do you say?" Emma smiled and nearly all the cells in my brain, heart and skin disassembled. It felt like everything in me and covering me got hair-raising goose pimples around her these days and I was questioning my integrity. *Oh shut up*…a voice inside me said. *You're just going up a ski lift.*

Once on the lift, Emma and I rode up the mountain, our legs dangling off the edge of our seats and the metal bar pressed to the top of our thighs. We both held on and watched as we were lifted into the sky and the space between our asses and the ground instantly rose several hundred feet, or so it seemed. I ogled a few climbers struggling with their footing.

Finally, I broke the silence. "Your mother has a love-hate relationship with my brother. Recently, she's taken to binding his book and trying to dance into my life like she suddenly likes me, too. Just the other day, she actually asked me if I wanted a Tarot reading. She's never said three sentences to me that were kind."

Emma shifted in her seat and gazed to the left of the mountain. "Mom's very much misunderstood. She's got a great heart but was burned terribly by my stepfather. He treated her with scorn and contempt and she spent most of her time just trying to protect me from him and his wrath."

"Did he hit her?"

"No."

"You?"

"No. He just yelled and never gave either one of us any room to be. I just remained the quiet watcher because I was sure I didn't really exist."

"Emma Jacobs. Really?"

"Really."

"Well, you exist..." The ski lift bumped then stopped. It sometimes did this, and we were now both sitting as high as you could get. "You wanna jump?"

"Blair, now who's the crazy one?"

"I heard that if you took a leap of faith you were either caught or taught how to fly. Think that'll happen here?" I smiled.

"I think you'll die."

"Dying wouldn't be so bad, then I wouldn't have to feel all of this anymore." I stumbled over the last word and looked off to the right, away from Emma's gaze. She put her hand on my hand on the rail. Luckily, my shoes were laced. My heart strings were the ones coming undone. It was so corny, weird and sad.

Emma spoke finally. "Mary Louise Martinez didn't have a chance. She's becoming another gay martyr like all those boys who killed themselves last year. God, I think it was eight or nine kids that either hanged themselves or shot themselves in the head and they were just the ones who got media attention. It's just different this time because it's a girl and we're a popular small tourist town and we haven't had as any of those hit the national spotlight. I've spoken to two reporters from the *Chicago*

Tribune. They're following the case, blogging about it, and next thing you know, we'll be on the talk show circuit."

"Can you handle that?"

"No. Could you?"

"No. Let's jump!" I laughed and she laughed and then the ski lift tossed and burbled a bit and sped us forward to the top. "You think Aaron's going to be okay?"

"I've been praying for him."

"Oh, no. Don't use that one."

"Blair, don't knock it till you try it. Prayer is underrated." Emma hit my shoulder.

"Ow. God doesn't exist. It's all science. How can you believe in God when the son of a bitch hasn't shown himself in, what?"

"Two thousand years?"

"Right. You know it better than I do," I laughed.

"Aaron's going to be all right, I think." We finished our ascent to the top of the mountain and prepared to get off the lift.

"Well, let's hope so!"

"Hope. Now, you're talking. Hope rhymes with Pope."

"Shut up, Emma!"

"You shut up, Blair." We both launched our asses off and I immediately felt a little high from the syrup on my dinner, pancakes and the altitude of the mountain.

Once we dragged up to the ridge, you could see Teton National Forest off the mountain's backside and the town of Jackson to the side we'd just come from. The restaurant looked like a relic from prehistoric lumberjack times. I placed my hands on my hips and watched Emma move forward away from me. A vibe was in the air but I had to ask anyway.

"Emma, are you straight or gay or bisexual or intersex or what. My guess is that you're straight but I don't have a clue."

"Why should it matter to put a label on any sexuality?" she asked.

"Because it separates the dykes from the femmes. The queens from the bears, the twiddle-dee-dees from the twiddle-dee-dots. I don't know. Straight. Gay. It seems to scream out loud who you really are."

"Or who you aren't. Bisexuals must have it the hardest. They have the entire Internet to surf. I'm just attracted to the person—whether they have a penis or a vagina does not matter. It's what's here." She patted her chest.

"Speaking of God. Oh my God. That is the cheesiest thing I've ever heard. I might vomit right here on the spot. Aren't you more attracted to one sex more than the other?"

"You know what I wanted you to see, Blair Underwear?"

"Now you're just pissing me off."

"Watch. Come closer." Emma in her light red jacket and her soft jeans stepped onto a pathway of a trail near the edge of the mountain closest to town.

She hoisted her pants up and reached into her back pocket to pull out a ponytail holder. She put it in and adjusted her hair through it and then stretched her arms out wide in the wild Wyoming air.

"Emma?" I asked. "Emma…what are you doing?"

Then without notice or warning, Emma did an entire cartwheel right there on the path in front of me. She landed in a backwards round off.

"You get a sex, I mean a six, from the drunk Irish judge!" But before I could manage the words issuing from my lips, Emma faltered. She slipped backward on the edge of the downslope and the Oh that formed on her mouth mimicked the Oh that was forming on mine. Her arms did a complete Ferris wheel apoplexy and she fell down backward butt first then head, then legs, and did the terrible tumbles downhill for some twenty yards or more as I slow-motioned my way to the edge myself. Once there, I lost my own footing and fell face-first into the dirt. My ankle still sore and stiff from the week before, I managed to fall and then slide face-first down to within three yards of Emma. I tried to get up and then farted.

"Ha, ha, ha. I heard that." Emma got up and tumbled down again.

The mountain was so steep it was hard to keep your footing going downward because the pitch was so steep. It felt like an almost vertical slope, give a degree or two.

Back down on my ass, I tried to reach for Emma but the

laughter erupted and we couldn't stop. My lungs burned laughing fire into my chest and I could see the snot on Emma's nose.

"Wipe your nose, you snotty lawyer God lover, you!" I yelled.

She hit me again in the other shoulder and I fell again. This time dirt went down my pants and I was upside down on the mountain: my feet facing the ridge at the top, my dirty hair heading to the bottom.

"Blair, I'm sorry," she said and held her hand over her mouth and laughed and inched her way toward me. "Here, let me help you up. You poor thing."

She reached down and I clasped my hand in hers. The first hard physical contact I'd had with her since the desire for her had begun. My palm was sweaty and so was hers and we slipped in our handy embrace till she reached farther down and grabbed my elbow with her other hand. After she pulled me up, we both leaned back a bit and faced the cartography, the topography of the town, the surrounding mountains and the range of the Tetons beyond route 29 and to the Northwest. My stomach dropped and Emma put her hands in the air.

"God, this is a powerful place, eh?"

"When the tectonic plates collided a trillion years ago, it must have clashed and clacked and rumbled beneath the ocean and rose up in a mystical way like the Stonehenge of the West," I said and let go of her hand.

"Let's get some coffee and go see Aaron. What do you say?" Emma smiled at me and for a moment I was reminded of a time years earlier when her eyes had locked in on me in an outbuilding of the Mystic Market, trying to save a dog with an old box of Cheerios.

"First I need to bandage up that knee of yours—" I said.

Emma leaned into me. "I need to bandage that cut by your eye near your temple. Nice scratch."

I reached to feel the pain or the blood. I wiped a bit of blood on my hand and then on my pant leg. "To my bungalow then. No flirting, Emma. If you flirt with me, then I might have to kiss you and then your mom will kill me."

"We're not kissing, Blair. And, my mom is not going to kill you."

"Then who is?" I smiled.

"You." She smiled back.

My, my, my. Emma tilted her head to one side trying to see what I might say next. Finally, I just motioned with my finger down the mountain and we began our journey on the same path, the same trail I'd taken as a kid. Blair Underwear. Holy agnostic. This was tilting in my thoughts as I could feel Emma's energy gently push me forward in a zigzag direction down the mountain.

An hour later, we were back at my bungalow. I retrieved my first-aid kit from my bathroom and let Emma make coffee.

"What I really need is a beer," I said and then pulled out a chair at the kitchen table. My screen door was open and you could hear the lashing crashing sounds of Cache Creek swirling around the graceful bends it created in its natural simple grandeur. I could hear swallows and firebirds whipper.

"I need to get home and do some work for the case." Emma sat down with the coffee and milk.

"Put your leg up here on my thigh," I commanded. She obliged and blew the steam from the top of her mug. My hands trembled as I poured a bit of peroxide on the gash on her knee. Holding some gauze to the edge of her skin, I carefully caught the tendril-like streams of liquid as I delicately watched the burst of white sizzling fume cover the moist blood. "It's like a science project," I said stupidly.

"Ah, that's nice. Thank you. You're a real medic, eh?"

"Yeah, you have to be in order to wear the cool brown uniform with the silver star."

Emma smiled and then I placed some ointment on a large Band-Aid and covered up the gash.

"Here, you next." She grabbed the kit and put her leg down. "Lean forward so I can take a closer look at that cut near your eye. Makes you look like you're an extra rugged cop."

"That's what I'm going for." I smiled and leaned in and then my legs started to shake uncontrollably. Up and down like they were Pop-Tarts in a manic toaster—up and down, down and up.

"Oh, my," I said. "This is embarrassing."

Emma put both hands on top of my legs and held them down and regarded me. I couldn't hear anything, couldn't see anything but her large blue eyes only inches from me. The whole world spun backward on its axis and the flow of time and space and the flutter and flap of butterflies and birds all halted. Right now. Right here.

She leaned in and softly, like with butterfly pressure, kissed the side of my neck. My heart hit her left shoulder, I was sure. Of the six million follicles of hair on my body, all stood up at once and sent an electric impulse that started at what Diana said was my crown chakra all the way to my root chakra. "Oh, my," I said.

She pulled away and our foreheads came together. "This is called the forehead prayer," she whispered.

Time stood still.

"I have to go," she said.

"My legs stopped jerking," I said calmly.

"This is good. We wouldn't want you to be a jerk." She laughed and I laughed.

Then I leaned in a little to see what might happen next and she stood up. "Big day in court tomorrow."

My cell phone suddenly started ringing. "It was a big day today…"

I answered the phone. It was Margie.

"Blair—" On the other end of the phone I could hear Mick talking. To whom, I could not tell. "Blair, can you hear this?"

After picking up her bag, Emma moved toward the front door. She waved.

"Ooooooo, barracuda," came the lyrics jamming out of the speakers of the iPod Mick had brought to Aaron. "We think he may be rousing! Get your skinny ass over here. Are you getting laid? We thought you'd be here an hour and a half ago!"

I waved to Emma to stay but she mouthed, "See you later," and then put her hands together in a prayer and bowed and walked out.

"None of that Namaste crap, missy!" I yelled after her as I watched her beautiful body cascade surreally away from my bungalow.

"What?" Margie asked at the other end of the phone.

"See you in court tomorrow!" I yelled to Emma who then put her hand up in a backward wave.

Margie kept interrupting. "What are you talking about? Who's there with you?"

"Emma Jacobs is now leaving. She stopped by for a cartwheel show, a ski lift ride and some ambivalent sexual behavior." I laughed.

"Get over here, now. You gob-smacking loser. Emma Jacobs would never kiss you in a million years," Margie yelled into the phone.

"She just did, Margie Hostetler, she just did. But, not on the lips."

"Where then, on your outstretched princess hand?"

"No, on my neck."

I could hear Margie talk to Mick. "Emma just kissed Blair Underwear on the neck."

The squeaker squeaked out, "Does this mean Emma's moving in and they're getting a kitten, a puppy and comfortable matching shoes?"

Margie cackled. "Did you hear that Underwear?"

I ignored her. "I'll be over in ten minutes. Just need to finish buying the wedding bands and getting a band of choristers from Provincetown to come out here and sing. One kiss on the neck and let the hitching begin. Mick needs to kiss you on the neck."

"She has. I mean we did. It that is. We did it. But we decided we still wanted boys instead. Jesus, sex is confusing isn't it. Especially after a joint, a bottle of vodka and listening to the Allman Brothers. We got a sense of longing for the past two years ago and ended up in the sack. Women aren't half bad. Mick and I had a good time."

"Oh...stop. I can't stand the thought of you-all together over an old Allman Brothers song from nineteen seventy-six. Geez. I'll be there shortly."

I hung up and went to my bedroom. I sat on my cinderblock bed and, once again, looked into the old mirror. The cut near my right eye was about an inch long and down the side to the top of my cheek. It wasn't deep and didn't hurt much. I did look extra rugged. I sat up straighter and then it occurred to me deep inside to my soul chakra, if there was an enemy, then it was me.

I was the enemy.

A revelation. In the worst kind of way.

CHAPTER TWELVE

Aaron lay still in his ghastly repose and his bed smelled of urine. Mick moved out of the chair next to him when I walked in and Margie closed the door partway. I put the back of my hand on his face and gently stroked his cheek. *Ole brochacho.*

"He seemed to rouse a bit when we played some of his music but now he's just back to the usual." Margie stood next to me and her tattooed arm rested on my shoulder. "Mick and I are going back to the Mystic to get something to eat and Mick's letting Fannie do a reading on her. It's Mick's gift to the lunatic fringetta." She smiled.

Aaron's eyes moved. "Aaron?" I whispered.

Mick moved to the other side of the bed. "Need another song, buddy?" Then ever so slightly, a smile seemed to alter his comatose countenance.

"Jesus, Mick," Margie nudged her, "put another one on by Coldplay. I think he liked the last one."

"I've been a bad sister," I blurted out. "Terrible. I should have taken him to the doctor on his last headache rampage but I didn't. I thought he just needed to lie down and take it easy. He's always driving all over town and going to the rec center and—"

Margie interrupted. "He's just living his life, girl. You've got no control over what he wants to do. He's just racing like the wind in that chair of his. He always has and always will. He loves to write. Mick, hand me his journal that Fannie bound for him. Have you read any of this?"

Mick slid over to the table by the window and grabbed the leather-bound manuscript. She handed it to Margie and then pulled her cigarettes from her purse and quietly walked out the door. "Maybe we can play him a tune in a bit," Margie said and picked up her BlackBerry and peered at it. A nurse walked by with a clipboard in her hand and the oxygen whirred in the room as well as Aaron's heart monitor.

Margie opened the journal and sat down in the chair next to mine. She turned to a page she'd bookmarked and cleared her throat and began to read.

"In my town, there is a place called the Mystic Market. Every day, I walk down there with my sister and we have breakfast before going to work. My sister is the town sheriff and keeps the peace most of the time. I am the newest rock star in town and have my own studio. I play lead guitar and sing songs I've been creating in my head for what seems like a million years. I sing like Axel Rose and play the guitar like a cross between Hendrix and Paige. Sometimes when I'm on stage, I gyrate my hips like Elvis used to in the fifties and sixties. I wear black leather and have an Indian feather in the back of my hair. My body is muscular and tan and the girls in the front row drool all over me. I am the King of Drool to some. My sister worries that I'll get a swollen head with all the attention from my adoring fans and that I'll blow all the money I make on cars, booze, women and trips to places where I can swim in blue oceans and drink drinks with tiny umbrella hats and garnishments that make it look like they were made in some resort pasture of heaven. I tell her that I'll only fool around for a year and

then she can quit her job of locking people up in jail cells, prison cells and we can go anywhere she wants. I want her to be happy because she has cared for me and my life for so long it hurts to watch her hurt for me anymore. I am sorry I've been such a burden on her by me trying to be the best brother in the world and a rock star all at once. I can't help if it if I sing like a bird and have a million people watching me on YouTube, Facebook and Entertainment Tonight.

"*When Ann and Nancy come to town to sing with me, I will tell them to bring my sister onstage because she can sing pretty good, too. Not as good as Nancy but near enough to sound all right. This is my burgeoning reality. I only use the word burgeoning because my creative writing teacher is hot and put a caret in the page where I write this and told me the word was a possibility, like all words, I suppose.*"

Margie sniffled. "Jesus Christ, what do you say to that?" Her tears hit the top of the page she was reading. My tears welled at my lower lids—a burn I'd never felt before. And I put my hand to my mouth before I fell apart right there in the hospital room, right there in front of my brother. I grabbed his silver IV pole and stood.

Margie stood. We embraced and my whole body shook in a convulsive wave of pain that intermixed with the reality of what he had said, what he meant, and why he was the best sibling on the planet.

"You haven't done anything wrong, Blair. He's sick. He's just sick. That's all, honey. You can't hold onto to his holding on. It does him no good. Just let go a bit. Let go. Let it all go and breathe for the first time in your life. Come on, you big pansy." Margie laughed and I laughed through a nice round of tears and blathering.

"Here." Margie handed me the journal. "There's more but I'm hungry and need a cocktail. I told your dad I'd have one with him at the Mystic."

"Margie. Thank you. You're a good friend. A really good friend. Even though you slept with a midget."

"Sounds like you might be sleeping with someone soon. Be careful or you might get that brother of yours jealous." She high-fived me in a girly way and missed my hand completely.

"She kissed me here." I touched my neck in the place where just a while ago, Emma Jacobs had placed her warm lips. Zing. My body reacted again and I blushed.

Margie put on her light brown leather jacket and extracted her hair from behind its collar. She pulled lipstick from her purse and drew the red shimmer across her lips. "Well, you're cute, Blair…in that T-shirt, jeans, comfortable-shoes-dyke way. Who wouldn't want to kiss you. You're too skinny, but the uniform does do something for me. But, I gotta have the dick. I like the dick more than the puss."

I threw my head back and laughed and then let my eyes fall on Aaron. Come on, *brochacho*—come out of this coma. I unclasped Aaron's cross from his neck and placed it in my pocket.

"See you later?"

"I'll be home by midnight. Court again tomorrow."

"Okay, we'll have smoked all the weed by then with our large hookahs." Margie scooted out the door.

The sister I never had.

I fingered the cross in my pocket and stayed as long as I could stand it.

CHAPTER THIRTEEN

Several witnesses testified in the morning before the key witness was summoned.

"All rise," the bailiff called the court to order in the afternoon and the Honorable Joe Archer returned to the judge's bench. The tension was taut like a tightrope once again and I glanced at Emma's patched up knee as she stood and called the next witness: Millie Palonski. The coach of the basketball team.

This was Mary Louise's moment, I thought.

She was nearly six feet tall and lanky, her hair was thin and long. Her face was gaunt and her eyes were those of a deer in headlights, humongous orbits. Oneida escorted her up and swore her in.

"...so help you, God," Oneida intoned.

"I do." And she took her seat in the witness stand chair. Her butt hit hard and she looked apprehensively at Emma.

"Your Honor, I'd like to also at this time introduce into evidence the suicide note found in Ms. Martinez's mouth on the day she was found." Emma held up a baggie and all could see the note inside. A reverent hush passed itself through the courtroom. I stood near the jurors and watched their reaction as I shifted my weight to my right foot and felt the leather of my belt. I slid my hands behind my back and watched Emma carefully, still feeling the vibration of last night mix in a bizarre way with vibration of the trial underway.

Mr. and Mrs. Martinez's heads went down at the mention of the piece of evidence being introduced. Mrs. Martinez picked up her rosary and began to count her prayers. Counting over and over again, pinching each bead between her thumb and index finger.

"Now, Mrs. Palonski, you have been the basketball coach of the Teton High School basketball team for how long?" Emma asked.

She shifted in her seat and looked at the jury. "Nearly sixteen years," she said, clipped and pithy.

"And how long have you been employed with the school system?"

"The same amount of time. I've been a coach and gym teacher."

"So, sixteen years." Emma looked down at her notes.

I put my hand to the cut from the previous evening and smiled, then caught myself at the irreverence.

"That's what I said."

"In the time that you were coach, have you always had the policy about alcohol and drugs and lesbians?"

"Objection." Virgil Steele stood up and his cowboy hat fell to the floor. "Your Honor, this line of questioning..."

Judge Archer put his hand up. "Virgil, I'll allow it. Have a seat." He then closed his eyes and told Emma to proceed with a flip of his wrist.

"Mrs. Palonski? Do you need me to repeat the question?"

There was a slight pause and then Millie Palonski said, "No, I have not had this policy in place."

She had just flat-out lied.

"Really? We have testimony from several players and two others on the faculty plus the resource officer that corroborate the fact that you had this policy in place."

"I did have a policy in place. It was strictly no drugs and no alcohol."

"No lesbians?"

"Yes. I mean no." She fought for the next word. "No drugs. No alcohol. Period." She eyed her attorney and he regarded her impassively.

"So, what you are telling me is that the other players who have testified are complete liars. Is this correct?"

Virgil Steele stood. Before he could say, "Objection," Archer waved him down.

"Yes, I mean no." Millie Palonski leaned forward and rocked back a bit. "I mean, they're just wrong."

"Mrs. Palonski, can you describe your relationship with Mary Louise Martinez?"

"Objection," Virgil called from his chair.

"Withdrawn," Emma said.

She turned toward the jury and walked that direction. I stood a bit taller and stared at the judge while keeping her in my peripheral vision. She addressed the judge but looked at the jury. "Your Honor, now that the suicide note has been introduced, I'd like to have the coach read it to the court. Mrs. Palonski you could do that for the court and the Martinez family, correct?"

Millie looked at her husband in the back of the courtroom, and the court reporters were scribbling madly on their legal pads. "No, I'd rather not."

"Do you know, Mrs. Palonski, that Mary Louise Martinez was a good student?"

"Yes, she was an A-B student. I took it upon myself to check all my players' academic records. She was no different."

"Oh, but she was. With your permission, Your Honor, I'd like to have Mrs. Palonski read this note."

Until now, no one except the people who worked in evidence and the attorneys had seen the note. All eyes were on the plastic baggie. My heart felt heavy and I kept seeing the tendrils of the basketball net frame the crown of Mary Louise's hair. Emma walked to the table and put her hand on the back of Mrs. Martinez who was already sniffling. Mr. Martinez leaned his shoulder into hers.

"Your Honor." Virgil Steele stood. "I want the jury to know that this note was typed at Mary Louise Martinez's home before she got onto school premises."

"As stipulated. Yes, go ahead, Ms. Jacobs."

Virgil checked his fingernails then closed his eyes.

Emma approached Millie Palonski and placed the baggie on the wide railing in front of her. "Please proceed."

Millie Palonski exhaled loudly. Her hands quivered as she picked up the clear plastic baggie and then cleared her throat.

"Please, if you will, Mrs. Palonski speak into the microphone." Emma glanced at the jury and stepped over to the Teton County Board side of the room near where Virgil was sitting.

"'*Dear Mom,*'" Millie blurted out and Mrs. Martinez cried out audibly. Her husband put his arm around her and she shook. The courtroom seemed a haze of hush you couldn't cut with a hatchet.

Millie looked up.

"Go ahead, Mrs. Palonski," Emma insisted.

"*Dear Mom and Dad,*

"*I am sorry for what I am about to do, so please don't be mad with me. You and Dad have raised me to be a good Catholic daughter, a good student. This is not your fault. Nor is it Miguel's or Juan's or Rosa's fault. Lately, the world here has pushed me in. I feel like the life of me has been squelched by the words of the players on the team and our coach. I am mystified that while the numbers on the calendar say 2011, that we still live like it's 1900. The Bible is still used as a weapon—just ask Father Mark.*

"*I feel isolated, tortured and alone. And, today, my life will end because of it. I can no longer stand the silence, the hatred, no one listening to me or seeing me for who I am. I've tried to tell people but no one listens. Why doesn't anyone listen anymore? Everyone just feels their own feelings and beliefs and I'm sick of competing with a world that sucks the life out of me with hatred and anger and all that when all*

I want is to love like a girl on a basketball team should love. I love the sport, the ball, the coach...especially her. But I can't love her anymore because she's married and has kids and I would ruin all of that. Well, I don't want to ruin her or anyone. I love her. I love her. It has all ended though. They all say it's impure and unnatural. All I know is that it's too confusing for me to take anymore.

"*Does anything even matter anymore? My teammates all know what's been going on but they stay silent too. The signs spoken and unspoken have infiltrated me and my head for nearly four years now. I have no last will and testament except to say that I will hang myself in a place I love, in a place where I fell in love, with a rainbow peace flag from—a gift sent to me from my AAU coach from Canada two years ago.*

"*I no longer want to be here among the people who hate who I am. I want to go to a place where people don't care about my personal life, a place where I can shoot baskets and kiss girls and feel safe. I want to go home—sooner than later because this world is too much to bear. I will miss you Mom and Dad. I will miss you. But the madness has to stop. Tell the world in your own quiet way that the madness has to stop.*"

Millie Palonski paused and turned the baggie to its backside. "Go on," Emma said.

"*I'm sorry to do this. Please know that till you come home to see me in heaven that I will be an angel on your shoulder, a whisper in your ear, a hand cradling your head whereever you may go. That's it. I love you all. Mary L.*

p.s. Please tell the world that when I see Nonno, Nanny, Uncle Bill and Matthew Shepard, and the boys from last year who did the same: Asher Brown, Seth Walsh, Justin Aaberg, Tyler Clementi, Billy Lucas, and all the rest that I will stomp on front porches and ring bells everywhere. We will be free. This, as they understood, is the only way out. A reasonable way out of all of this.

"*p.p.s. Tell Rosa she can have my bike. My brothers can have my computer and Nintendo. Teton High School can have the flag around my neck.*"

Millie Palonski's lips quivered on the last part and she shoved the note back toward Emma.

The courtroom erupted with chatter and the judge pounded his gavel forty-two times it seemed and demanded order in the court. Oneida stepped forward and put her hands in the air to shush the naysayers and people who were elbowing each other and flapping their respective jaws. My jaw was opened a bit more, I think it was the line about the stomping on the porch and the ringing of the bells.

Jesus Christ. And, then I was amused that I thought of him. I was beginning to wonder if my Gnostic brain was becoming re-wired. *Hell no, hold on to your beliefs, dummy.*

I shook it off…what was wrong with me?

I assisted Oneida in the shushing and Judge Archer again slammed his hammer down. Emma took the baggie holding the note and brought it over to show the jury.

And held it high for everyone to see. The Martinezes continued to sob and the jury was noticeably affected. Two men shed tears. One juror just let her tears slide slowly down her face. Virgil Steele remained cool to his name.

Archer finally got everyone settled and addressed Emma. "Counsel, any further questions?"

Emma stood up. "I think the note answered most, Your Honor. For now, at least."

"A simple yes or no will do, Ms. Jacobs," he scolded. "Mr. Steele, you're up."

Virgil took the note from Emma and approached the witness stand. "Mrs. Palonski. Is this the first time you've seen this note?"

"No sir."

"When did you first see this note?"

"When you showed it to me at the police station."

"And, this is the same note?"

"Yes."

"Now, Mrs. Palonski. Are there any specific words in here that state that you and Mary Louise Martinez were having an intimate, physical affair?"

"No, I don't see anything."

"Where it says, 'in a place where I fell in love,' is she referring to you?"

"No."

"Mrs. Palonski, the jury will want to know if you were having an affair with Mary Louise Martinez. Were you?"

She turned to them and in a preachy tone stated in slow matter-of-fact way, "I most certainly was not." She shook her hair around and pursed her lips.

"For the record, Your Honor, and ladies and gentlemen of the jury, there is no factual statement in this note that verifies that Mrs. Palonski was having an affair with Mary Louise Martinez. Indeed, this note appears somewhat delusional. Talking of angels, Matthew Shepard, and whispering into your ear after you are dead. Wouldn't you say so, Mrs. Palonski?"

"Objection! Counsel is putting words in Mrs. Palonski's mouth!"

"Sustained."

"No, counsel," Virgil addressed Emma. "I believe that Mary Louise put these words in her own mouth, right? Her own mouth, right?" Virgil barked. "A very sick, depressed young lady."

Emma put her hands on her hips and eyed Virgil Steele in withering contempt.

Virgil stayed steady. "Strike my last statement. Thank you. No further questions, Your Honor."

He slammed his hammer down again. "Court is recessed till nine a.m. Monday morning. I'd like to see counsel in my chambers. Now."

After the courtroom was emptied, Oneida came up to me. Her kids arrived with another sheriff. I texted Mick and Margie simultaneously that I wanted to do dinner somewhere in town, maybe the Cadillac Ranch. Away from it all. *Run. Run.*

Oneida asked quietly, "So, what did you think?"

"Emma is good but the note solidifies nothing, right?"

"I think it solidifies everything, Blair. Did you hear the hush? It seemed obvious to me that something was going on between the two of them. And, there's more evidence, a letter or something from Coach Palonski to Mary," Oneida said. "We catalogued a shoebox with letters into evidence just a few weeks ago when Rosa and her mother found them in the far recesses of Mary Louise's closet. All handwritten."

"God it sounds so Emily Dickinson." I grabbed some papers and a legal pad on the table for Emma. I saw that Mrs. Martinez had left her cross. I grabbed it and placed it carefully in my pocket. "Well, let's hope they help—all Teton County Schools has to do is prove that she was not right in the head. Perhaps they'll bring in the town psychiatrist, next. Who knows?"

Oneida put her arm around her son. Emma at the same time came marching out of the judge's chambers, her face set purposefully. She picked up her leather folio, shuffled some papers around and then marched through the courtroom doors to the reporters waiting on the other side.

I said quickly, "I'm going to shadow her, Oneida."

"Okay, I'll get Virgil's back when he comes out."

I hustled through the double doors and stood behind Emma as she gave a statement to the press. The air was warm and the perfume from some of the reporters wafted in the wind. The air smelled strange, a tincture of pine and mountain scent.

"Well," she stated. "We have good reason to believe that we will be triumphant over the Teton County School District in this suit. The Martinez family has been through a tragic, tragic event that could have been stopped. Anti-bullying measures are in place at the school but they were not enforced. They were blatantly ignored."

A reporter asked from the crowd. "We all heard the suicide note today and the question is will it be enough?"

Emma shifted. "It's plenty, especially with the testimony we have. We will prevail, I'm sure."

On the other side of the steps, I could hear Virgil bellowing out his billy jack boondoggle to the other side.

"Mr. Steele, do you feel that a school system should pay compensatory damages to everyone who gets bullied today from the fatties, to the uglies, to the gay, straight, bisexual, transgendered? Doesn't everyone get bullied? Do you envision lawsuits like this popping up all over the country?" The Fox reporter smiled as he asked his questions.

Virgil smiled back like a Republican Tommy Lee Jones. "They already are. Students are bullied and harassed for all kinds of reasons. Shoot, I was harassed at the University of Virginia for having a bit of a Midwestern drawl. But, back then and now, our parents and friends taught us how to have thick skin and to turn the other cheek. Seems to me we have a similar situation here. It's tragic but the school district acted appropriately. My clients have policies and measures in place that ensure that no one—let me repeat—no one, will be hurt, harmed or bullied on school grounds."

Another reporter asked, "But don't you think it might be a little naïve in this day and age to think that being harassed for a different accent can be compared to consistent harrassment?"

Virgil considered the reporter. "Well, I don't like your pantsuit. You look like you're squished into it funny and your hair looks like it could use an appointment with the hairstylist. Is that harassment, the truth, or me just being mean?"

The reporter lowered her mic and stared at him.

"Now, look," Virgil went on, "I'm just joking with you. But you get my point, right? Whatever happened to the First Amendment and freedom of speech? I see no clear and present danger here. The KKK didn't rally around the young girl's house and neither did a bunch of the Right Wing Christian Fred Phelps clan either. He's too busy causing mayhem at the funerals of our fallen soldiers. This is a clear-cut case of severe depression and suicide. Period."

A reporter from CNN called out, gesturing. "Have you looked over there, Mr. Steele?"

All eyes went to the small Westboro Church enclave set up a half a block down. Police tape surrounded them and they were the same demonstrators that I'd blipped my horn at several months earlier when we went to the cemetery. This time the signs were, "God hates Dykes," and "God hates Faggots," and "You're all going to Hell: Leviticus 18:22."

My eyes closed when I saw this and I reached into my pocket and pulled out the cross. For a moment, I was going to fling it into the wind but then I remembered it was not mine to fling.

An hour later, I was home and sitting in front of my mirror

as I unbuttoned my shirt. Maya my-poet-dog-buddy Angelou scratched at my screen door and I let her in. Her black hair was oily and her large paws clacked across my kitchen floor. I checked my phone as I scratched the back of her ears. There was a text from Emma asking to meet me at the sheriff's office.

It was getting late, but I rebuttoned my shirt, checked my hair in the mirror and texted her back that I was on my way.

When I got to the front door of the sheriff's office, I opened it to find Judd and Emma talking in his office. Something told me something was wrong.

Judd said without preamble, "Blair, we've got an issue with some evidence in the Martinez case. Emma came in to look over the letters and when I went to the evidence room to retrieve them, well, they're missing. The letters are gone." He hiked up his pants and a bead of sweat formed on his upper lip.

"You've got to be kidding. Who's working in evidence these days?"

"I'm certain Todd and Marty collected it and checked it in with Oneida and put it in the evidence room; but, I just went to get it for Emma, and I could not locate it." He wiped his fuzzy beard and put some chewing tobacco inside his lip.

"Who else has been coming in and out of here?" I asked.

Judd hung his head. "Just us and the attorneys—I'm assuming. This is going to be a difficult one to explain. I called you because you have most seniority in the department besides Frank and he's too busy eating doughnuts to care. I want to keep it between you and me and Emma for the moment but shortly, I'm going to have to call Virgil and let him know and the Martinez family too."

"This will throw the case, Judd," I said, numbly, scarcely believing what I'd just heard. "How can evidence for the most important case in this town's memory just go missing?"

"Did someone scan it?" Emma cogently asked.

"Our scanner is on order. It hasn't arrived yet," Judd said matter-of-factly.

She put her hands on her hips and thrust her face inches from his. "Jesus Christ, Judd. This isn't easy to swallow. You know what this means. My case against Teton County Schools and Palonski and Clarkson just flew out the window. We might not even have a case anymore. The suicide note isn't strong enough against her." Emma spun on her heel and sat in a huff on a nearby metal folding chair.

I wasn't sure at all what to do. Emma had to prove that on some level Teton County school system was at fault. "Who's been in the evidence room besides Marty or Todd or me or Oneida?"

"The cleaning lady, Ava Banks, and perhaps her daughter, who she sometimes brings in with her on her night shift till her Dad comes to get her." Judd said this and slumped down at his desk.

"Well." I put my hands in my back pockets and shifted my weight off my right ankle. "We're going to have to talk to them. The only other people who linger around here some are Ray and Fannie but neither has any sense to come in here after hours."

"You and Oneida go and check out Ava Banks and see if anyone else has been in here besides her and her daughter. Her daughter is either at the elementary school or the middle school. Check on that too." Judd spat tobacco into a red plastic cup.

It occurred to me then that Judd was on our side. Good man. Good, good man.

Emma buried her head in her hands and then angrily pushed her hair back. "I'm going home to get ready for trial tomorrow. Let me know what you find out, Blair. This is really upsetting. Without those letters, we're in pretty bad shape."

"Okay, I'll call Oneida, and we'll pay Ava a visit. If I find anything out, I'll either call or come by?"

There was a pregnant pause in the room.

Emma looked at Judd. Judd looked down at some papers on his desk. "I'll leave it to you, Blair. You look tired. Aaron okay?"

"I'm going to stop by the hospital with Oneida on our way to visit Ava and check. I'll fill you in later."

CHAPTER FOURTEEN

Mick met me at the front of the nurse's station with a large smile on her large midget face. "I've got a big, big surprise for you, Ms. Wingfield. You know I've had to pull some strings but this is a small miracle."

"What are you talking about, you Vienna sausage snickety snack? If you had sex with my comatose brother, I'm locking you up." I smiled and so did she.

Margie came out of Aaron's room into the hallway near an empty gurney and almost doubled over in laughter. Then she pointed at Mick and shuffled up to me and slapped me on the back. Two nurses told us all to keep it down in unison but even they began to giggle.

"What is going on and someone needs to tell me right now!" I yelled.

"Shut up, you wingless wombat. Christ! Come over here and I'll show you."

Margie led me to the door of Aaron's room and I peeked in with Margie and Mick over each shoulder till I thought we would all tumble into the room.

For a moment, I wasn't sure who the dark-and auburn-haired ladies were but the guitar being strummed ever so lightly by the auburn-haired lady was what gave it away, something I thought could never be true. An instrumental version of "Crazy for You" was being strummed for my brother and the singers were the real thing: Ann and Nancy Wilson. Ann and Nancy Freaking Wilson were singing to my brother in a small hospital, in a resort town in the middle of the summer of his and my life. My jaw dropped in suspended disbelief. My stomach went furling out in front of me and suddenly I could not breathe. I was starstruck and dumbstruck at once.

I turned to Mick who had been squeezing my hand and kissed her on the cheek, then I turned to Margie and did the same.

"Stop it you homo. We did it for him not for you." She slapped me on the back.

I asked Mick, "How did you pull this one off?"

"I've known them a long time. When you're in the music industry and looking for acts, it's good to talk to the people and to know the ones who've been around the longest. These gals are a class rockin' act all the way around. We're friends."

"I can't believe it," I said.

"Believe it, you atheist carpet muncher, the Wilson sisters have got you wondering, eh?"

"What, divine intervention?" I asked.

"No," Mick interjected. "Heart...totally and completely." She put her hand to her chest.

"Ah-ha. We have our play on words!"

We all three stood there watching as they sang. I gazed at Aaron, wondering if any of it was getting through to him. *Come on, brochacho. You've got to make it. I can't do this life without you.* Margie listened for a second and then said, "Mick found out they were playing over in Boise at the Glen Allen Theater and they had a three-day break. They flew in just for Mick because they heard about Aaron and how much he loves them. So, great to know people in high places?"

We both stared at Mick and all of us laughed at the inadvertent pun.

"You are some sick wonderful people," I said. "What would I have done without you?"

"Go do your job, Blair Wear. We've got this handled…"

Hesitating momentarily, I peeked in and then walked in as they sang the chorus, "Crazy for You." I mouthed a thank you to both of them and swept the hair from Aaron's forehead and kissed him on the cheek. I then whispered in his ear, "You've got two hotties in your room by the name Ann and Nancy, your favorite band—Heart—you'd better wake up." When I observed his face, his jaw was slack and the oxygen tubes draped upward into his nose. His frailty was almost unbearable, but I grabbed his hand anyway and kissed him one more time. "I'll be back later for the recap. You better be awake so I can see those brown Hawking eyes of yours, bird man from Jackson Hole."

I turned and walked to the door, and bowed in a botched reverence to the famous sisters. They were cute and sang liltingly to Aaron. All I could think of was a beach where he could walk, write in his journal and drink drinks with tiny umbrellas. I longed for this for him.

I longed for this for me.

Oneida was in her pajamas when I got to her house on Silver Street and her kids were doing somersaults on the couch. Most of her charming byplay was "stop hitting your brother and sister." Nikki was ten and ruled the roost between Peter and Elena who were eight and five respectively.

"Do you want kids, Blair?"

"Do you?"

"Shut up. You can have these three for a small price." Oneida got two mugs from her cupboard and filled them with hot water for tea.

I sat on the barstool by the kitchen counter while pillows flew willy-nilly in the background. "What's the price?"

"I'll pay you half my weekly salary to take them to any of the outbuildings by the Mystic and drop them off. Between you and crazy Fannie, Diana and Aaron, you can all take care of them."

"Sure. When do you want me to abduct them?"

"Yesterday."

"Gotcha. I'll get Fannie onto it. She needs to be jailed anyway, which brings me to the reason why I'm here. Evidence is missing from the Martinez case. The letters. Besides you and Todd and me and Marty, who's been in the evidence area?"

"When did it go missing?" Looking shocked, Oneida sat next to me. Then she yelled. "Nikki, stop choking Peter. Elena, get over here and finish your dinner."

I scanned a plate of mashed potatoes, peas and turkey half eaten on a plate where four stuffed animals lined the plate as if they'd been staring at it too.

Little Elena came over with her blanket, a thumb in her mouth, and a pink butterfly clip in her hair. Placing her fork in the palm of her hand, she glanced sideways at her mom. Oneida gave her a silent look, and she put two peas on her fork and put them in her mouth.

"Peas. Really, Oneida?" I made a face at Elena and she smiled while reluctantly pushing her food in circles on the plate. "The evidence was noted as missing today when Emma wanted to take a look at it."

"Hmm." Oneida thought. "The only people even close to the evidence room would be us, Ava, and hmm…"

"Do you think Ava would have messed with it? I know she brings her daughter into the offices when she first comes in but there's always someone there. Either Todd or Marty or Judd or…" I trailed away pensively.

"Wait. Wait. Maybe it's Ray." Oneida set her coffee cup down, then wrangled Peter by his elastic waistband to get him away from Elena so she could eat. He reluctantly looked at me, I crossed my eyes, and he smiled.

"Ray? Ray White? What do you mean?"

Oneida let him go then said, "Well, he's always hanging

around the courthouse and he and Ava are pretty good friends. I see them walking around town sometimes, even down at the Mystic hanging around the outbuilding behind the market."

"Why would Ray or even Ava for that matter take evidence from the evidence room?"

Oneida turned to Nikki and told her to turn on the Cartoon Network for Peter. "Channel three twelve, Nikki. You know," she said, to me, "I bet you someone has given one of them money to take them and the only reasonable idiot would be either someone in the school system or Millie Palonski herself. We need to find those letters, Blair."

"Or the people who took them. I'll question Ava and Ray separately. Perhaps one of them will give it up. I can see Ray maybe, but Ava? Isn't she a God-squader like you and Emma?"

"Not all God-squaders are bad, Blair." Oneida tapped her head and exhaled heavily.

"Right, just the ones who stand behind the saccharin-sweet veil of his eternal importance. Jesus is such a good character to hide behind. Maybe I'll start doing it myself."

"How's Aaron?" Oneida said.

"Jesus. He's just fine."

"Shut up."

"You shut up."

Elena looked inquisitively at the two of us. "Is Jesus coming now, Momma?"

I looked at Oneida.

"No, honey. Not today. But someday, he'll be here. No worries. Blair, if you say anything sarcastic right now, I'll pistol-whip you into the next millennium."

I laughed. "Yes, Sergeant silverware." I saluted her then got off my stool and patted Elena on the head. "Jesus is everywhere from what I hear, Ms. Elena. But don't believe everything you hear."

Oneida stood up. "Out. Go find your villain, but I think if you look closely, you'll find it's yourself. You, Ms. Blair. Kiss Aaron for me. We'll say a prayer for him, right Elena?"

Elena smiled and nodded.

When I got to Ava's house fifteen minutes later, I rapped

quietly on the door. It was nearing the time when she would be going to the courthouse to do her cleaning and when she opened the door she looked as if she was getting herself together. As I walked in, I did what I normally do when I went into someone's home. I smelled the smells and then scanned. On the side table, there was mail, keys and candles lit under an altar for the Virgin Mary, I guessed. Homemade soup, or something homemade, was on the stove. Her house was tiny and looked as if she might be sharing it with someone else. Three pair of boots sat by the door and one was a man's pair. The kitchen was pristine with small soup bowls stacked neatly in a row on the Formica countertop. There were three small angels and a cross on the windowsill. In the living room, behind her couch on the wall were two old oil paintings of what looked to be nineteenth century people; unhappy in countenance, posing seriously for the painter.

"Ava, I have something I need to ask you," I said as she led me in. "Have you been the only one in the evidence room in the last two days after hours?"

Ava sat down on her couch. I guessed she must have been fifty pounds overweight. Her hair was up in a bun and her entire body seemed to soak into the couch as if she hadn't had a break in forty years. "Yes, Blair. I'm the only one in there. My daughter comes for a while but she sits in the desk up front doing her homework."

I stared at the pictures on the wall. "At no time was anyone else in there?"

"No, not that I recall. Let me think. Oh, wait. Fannie came by yesterday to drop off something for Emma and was there for a while but that was it."

"Did you see her leave, Ava? Did you see Fannie leave the station?"

Ava shook her head. "I don't know. I thought I saw her leave but I'm not sure. We talked for a bit and Todd and Marty were in the break room, I think. No, Todd was in Judd's office doing something. I don't know." She looked at me confused and a tiny bit defensive. "What's going on?"

"So, Fannie was there and you didn't see her leave. Is that what you're saying?"

"Yes."

I jumped up. "Thanks, Ava. I might have to ask you some more questions but you've got me on the right path."

"What—"

Out of Ava's house in a nanosecond, I jumped into my Jeep and called on the radio to Sheriff Williams that I had some new information on the possible suspect. I was elated, almost high with having some evidence.

"Deputy Wingfield to Judd, copy?" I called for him.

"Judd here, Blair, go ahead, copy," he said back, then sounded shaky on the "copy" part.

I ignored it. "Judd, I've got some information on who may have been in the office in the last few days, copy?" I spoke into my radio and clicked it.

"Uh, yes, Blair, I copy. But, right now, we need you down here at the Mystic to do some crowd control. Copy?" Judd sounded breathy.

"Good grief, are Ann and Nancy Wilson playing with Amy? Copy?" I smiled.

There was a slight pause. "No, Blair. It's worse, much much worse. The Mystic Market is up in flames."

The earth and wind and sky around me suddenly glazed over thick with time and terror. The Mystic Market on fire? What on earth? Oh my God! *Oh my God!*

"Is anyone hurt? Is there anyone in there? Copy?" My voice cracked in my throat and all I could see was Diana, Fannie, Maya, Ray, Tyler and anyone shopping, eating, reading or getting a card reading.

"We're doing a count now, the fire department is here. What's your ten twenty? Copy?"

But I had no words.

A vise came down on my head and I put my hand to my heart as I accelerated to a speed too high for a small, homey town. I flew by the church, passed the Cowboy Bar, passed the rodeo grounds in a circumlocution that had me completely lost. Circles, circles, circles. A bird hit my windshield. I could not see, I could not hear, the press of the world came down. If I were Atlas, I would have shrugged. I drove my Jeep fast but lost my direction, did not know where I was, nor who I was. A lady on the street hollered for me to slow down but her words just vibrated out into the air as if they hadn't even been said. My hands were clamped on the steering wheel. I saw Aaron. I saw Dad. I saw my mother sitting in Florida looking at her polished nails. I saw Emma tumbling down Snow King Mountain. I saw the Martinez family flash by on the hood of my Jeep as real as reality said it could be. I slammed on my brakes right in front of Teton High School's gymnasium. When I looked to my left at Cache Creek Canyon, I could see smoke billowing from the place where the Mystic was. The plumes of fire and smoke shot high in the sky and rolled their way up, up and up like a black oily peppery balloon. Above the mountains, it annealed itself to the blue sky and spread out like an upside down blanket to a place where it would orbit for miles and miles and miles. Placing my hand to my neck, I felt Mary Louise's presence there on the hood of my Jeep, the smoke, the blue sky and the setting sun. The Mystic Market's smoke circled the sun in a giant envelope and for the first time in my life I saw an eclipse.

Then I felt Aaron die.

My worst nightmare and my biggest miracle.

The smoke moved and I put the car in gear. Like a catatonic soldier back from war, I drove the speed limit toward the place I'd called home. I went past the hospital and saw blue wheelchair access signs everywhere. In my mind, I said to Aaron, "Fly my brother, fly."

The words issued from my lips as if another person were saying them.

"Go, Hawk, go."

CHAPTER FIFTEEN

Weirdly, when I got to the market, Diana was doing some gyrating gypsy dance around some of her psychic cronies and Fannie was doing the dirty dirge with her. They looked like really bad whirling dervishes, hypnotic in the blend of the light and night but I shrugged it off. They weren't hysterical as I'd imagined. When Diana laid eyes on me, she bolted over.

"Hey, you okay?" she asked.

"The market is up in flames and you're not whacked?" I said this as she stood there in front of me as the whole of the market billowed and went to ash in the air. Flakes of the embers littered the wispy wind around her face and mine.

Three fire trucks had their hoses flowing onto the Mystic. One truck was hosing down the bungalows so they wouldn't catch fire. Police officers and firemen were milling about keeping people away and focusing their energy on getting the chaos under control.

"He's dead, I think, Diana?" I whimpered and started to cry.

She put her arm around my waist and then Maya came running with a stick of wood in her mouth. She dropped it at my feet and sat next to Diana.

"The nurse and Mick and Margie, even the Wilson sisters, came down from the hospital to get you. They're over there with Emma." Diana pointed and my knees quaked.

I thought I would pass out. "Will you tell Emma to come over here?"

Diana looked at me lovingly, then she put her strong hands to my cheeks and held my head. "This is going to be the hardest thing for you to accept, you know—and I'm just not talking about Aaron dying, honey. Just feel it, Blair. Feel it for the first time in this life. It's this life, Blair. This one."

"Okay, I guess." It was the last thing I remembered saying before I surreally and slowly fell to my knees for the third time in as many months, the first being at the Catholic church getting coffee with Oneida the day after Mary Louise Martinez's death, the second was trying to resuscitate my brother in the middle of Lovely Road, and now I was down again, the dirt and flame all about. When Emma stood in front of me, the cells in my body burst into fire like the Mystic in front of me. I leaked out of myself and onto the ground as if my heart and lungs and liver and brain needed to spill out and leave my body organless to take a break from my own tragedy, my own forsaking.

Ever since I had been little, God had been nowhere. Now, like a waking dream, Emma was before me and I could feel the past regression of everything, all my past lives. A war in Rome, a kiss in Russia, a triumph in Taiwan, a memory of re-gendering in England, where Orlando met Virginia Woolf. I felt an Irish mystery and twist of fate when Emma was a man and I was a man and we lived near the Lake Isle of Innisfree where we had a small farm, sheep, and people thought we were distant cousins who had lost our families, lost our ways. To America where we'd miss each other because of parents and religious ideologies, but still I sat behind her in grammar school and thought of kissing her at recess behind the jungle gym. Sometimes I was a thief and angry and wrong. So, too, was she. We yelled but we didn't hit. In South America Emma had loved dogs and taught me to love them too. Especially shepherds. In Germany, a black dog in a long-forgotten cemetery lay over our Jewish bodies. Never famous, never the likes of any dukes or duchesses or kings and queens. Not pirates or villains or heroes of any sort. Just fighters for the common people, fighters for ourselves and the truth.

Simple as that.

"You were awfully cute a hundred years ago," I blurted out in a semi-conscious state to Emma.

"So were you. Thanks for showing up this time and finally having the courage. I see you have your star in the right place." She put her hand to my deputy's star over my heart. I put mine on hers. We clasped our hands together in an eternal lock that had no key.

Fannie came tumbling up. "Aaron can walk again. Finally. Took you forever to let go. Next time, you'll have some information here." She punched me lightly in the belly with her foot.

"You mean a gut instinct? I'm going to miss him. My brother. Oh, God, my brother! Emma…Emma…can we go to him?"

"Right now. Let's go right now. Never any time better than the present."

"I heard that," Diana said. "Blair, we've got insurance. I've paid the damn bills. No worries. We'll rebuild this place. This time it won't be like a Phoenix, the bird that rises from the ashes of fate. This time it will right what they got wrong all along. Those mythic assholes had it wrong all along."

"What's that?" I asked, wiping away the tears.

"It's many birds, Blair. It's many. Not just one phoenix. It's not just one, honey. It's hundreds of them." Diana grabbed Maya Angelou and walked over to Ray White and grabbed his flask and swallowed hard from it. "A little nip is going to help me through this one. Right, honey?"

Jesus, who were these people?

A voice inside my head said, *Your family.*

When we got to the hospital room, all the tubes were out of Aaron's body and he lay there like an angel. Emma held my hand and as I neared his body, I released her hand and grabbed his.

"I guess the Wilson sisters weren't the ticket, eh?" I asked.

Mick and Margie came in behind Emma. I could feel their presence. Margie came close to me and put her arms around me, cradling me.

"What bird are you?" I asked through my tears.

"I'm a big bird, dumbass. A lanky, big bird," she said.

Emma went to the other side of the bed and Mick sidled next to her. Mick grinned and said, "I guess this makes me Tweetie." We all laughed simultaneously. Aaron would have loved it.

"I'm going to miss you, you Stephen Hawking goober." I swallowed hard and then regained my lungs in a spasm. I put my head on his shoulder and we all stayed with him for what seemed an eternity.

And, I guess it was.

When I returned to the Mystic with Emma a few hours later, I saw the smoldering ruins across the grounds but the firemen had saved all but one bungalow. The outbuilding where we'd saved the dog once had magically survived and Fannie was behind it digging up the earth.

"She loves to plant," Emma said. "She's been wanting to plant a garden behind that building as long as I can remember."

"Should we help?" I said, holding onto her arm.

"No. Time for you to go rest. I'm walking you home to your bungalow and sleeping on your couch. Mick and Margie are coming back with some food. As I recall your refrigerator is always empty."

"I'm no cook. I'll own that one." I smiled.

"I'm not either. Guess we'll starve to death without the Mystic's kitchen to keep us alive."

"Emma?" I asked.

"Yes," she said.

"Kiss me, please. I've been waiting a long time."

In front of the burnt Mystic and my small bungalow and out in the street, Emma grabbed my right hand and then my left and then stared at me with her magical ice-blue eyes. "You sure you can handle me?"

My knees jerked involuntarily. "Please…"

But before I could say the rest and disgust myself and make a debacle of things, I let her put her forehead to mine then her nose then her soft smooth lips caressed mine. When her tongue parted my lips I felt the pulse from my throat to my nipples to the blood coursing to the hot spot between my legs. The veracity of it—the sensation intensified in a cadence, a song I'd never quite imagined. But then again, in the face of my brother's death, I'd never been so quite alive. Here she was. The smart lawyer from Yale who had little to say in saving me from my own dumbass life, as Margie would say. We kissed to the right. We kissed to the left. We kissed for almost five minutes solid till Diana parted us and told us to go inside.

We did. Emma Jacobs chapped my lips on the worst day of my life.

She held me on the couch all night and when I would awake to the knowledge that Aaron was gone and silently sob, she would hold me tighter and whisper in my ear that it was okay. He was free.

The funeral arrangements were easy. All Aaron ever wanted was to be at the Mystic but now that the Mystic was burnt to heaven as Mick put it, we had to make different arrangements. So, Diana and Dad and I got together and decided we'd make something pretty behind the market. Fannie and Ray White put up a trellis and the people from the rec center and Flapper Jack's came and brought me tuna casseroles, chicken casseroles, meatloaf, scalloped potatoes, a beef brisket and flowers. His buddies from the basketball team brought homemade beer that

Aaron had drunk on occasion and the basketball Aaron had played with, their names scribbled all over it. The guys from where Aaron played poker brought cigars and cards and sat around my kitchen table and got drunk with Dad.

On the evening of the third day after his death, my mother came all the way from Florida wearing a floral pantsuit. She came in, hugged me briefly, and immediately told me my hair was too short and where were Aaron's things.

"Blair, I know I haven't seen you in over a year. I'm sorry about Aaron." She said this, put her hands to her face and convulsed a cry, and then flopped into one of the chairs at the kitchen table.

"Hey, Mom, just when I'd almost given up on being an atheist...well, here you are. You want a beer, or a Valium or some crystal meth?" I asked contemptuously, yet I was somewhat glad to see her.

"Watch your mouth, Blair. I'm not too old to take that pistol from your belt and knock you over the head."

A moment later, my dad came in through the screen door. "Hey, Rosie," he said to Mom. "Long time no see. You doin' okay?" He stood there waiting for a response.

Mom went to the cupboard looking for a cup. "I'm fine David. How's your girlfriend? What number are you on now thirty? Forty?"

"I'm glad to see you still have your biting tongue," he said then winked at me.

I smiled at my father. "Listen, you two, sit here and play friendly catch-up, but I need to get out of this place and go to work for a while. I've been in this bungalow for three days while people bring me things I can't eat. Look at all of this." We all scanned my counters covered with trays of food and drink and flowers.

"This town loved Aaron, Blair," Dad said and took off his hat. "He was a good boy...kind..." He trailed off then his lips quivered. "I remember when we brought him home from Rock Springs and that first Christmas. He could already walk. Blair you read to him from every book you could lay your hands on. Remember that?"

I nodded and Mom sat down. Her hair was in a large clip and her lipstick slightly askew. She smiled at me and bit into a doughnut. She inhaled it almost as fast as I could get to my next thought.

"I remember you and Mom and Aaron letting Patches slide Aaron down Hansen Street in that sled you concocted, Dad. Remember that?" I stood up to crack my neck and stretch. "We all let them fly down the street and Aaron laughed…" I put my hands to my face like Mom had just done to hers.

My mom got up. "Oh honey, it's okay…God's got Aaron in the palm of his hands." She came to me and wrapped her arms around me.

"What happened to you?" I asked, pulling away roughly.

"Paxil and the Pope…well, back to church at least. I'm better, Blair. Just not perfect like everyone wanted me to be."

Dad took a seat and grabbed a doughnut. "Paxil and the Pope…going back to church, eh, Rosa?"

"There's a nice Catholic church that I've come to like, yes," Mom admitted.

I said, "Well, goody for you."

I went to the bathroom a tad pissy and washed my face and neck. When I returned a few minutes later, Mom and Dad were holding hands across the table. As I appeared, they released their grip.

"I'm going in to see how Emma is faring at the trial."

I marched through the screen door in my deputy's uniform and was again jolted by the char that was once the Mystic Market. Six or seven men from a crew of workers were putting the flotsam and jetsam into a large trailer bin and a construction worker was talking to Diana while Maya dug up the dirt behind the old market where Fannie was planting with several women from the rec center. They were making it look nice for the service neither Aaron nor I would want, but it was the town that wanted it and I was too tired to argue with any of them. I was tired of them, of my family, of the battle with God or no God.

I was still convinced that God had some form of hellish OCD-like behavior. Doesn't God have a flat screen, I wondered. Doesn't the Universal Consciousness of the Now, the It, the

Oversoul have the ability to see the highlights from the *Today Show?* If God is all That, then I didn't want any of all that. It was too hard to believe when the war inside of all of us was just as bad as any war existing on the outside of us. He wasn't there when Aaron was hurt on that trampoline, nor was he there when Ann and Nancy showed up to play for him on his death bed. Distracted and obsessed, again, over someone or something far, far away was all I could assume God was in a belief I held real.

Mick stopped me in the middle of my catharsis. "Blair Wear, you think we should get Father Mark to say a few words at Aaron's funeral?"

I grabbed her by her shirt. "Mick, do you see me?"

"What?" she shivered.

I raised her up a bit. "Do you see me?"

"Yes, Blair. I see you."

Margie came out from their rented bungalow. "Put her down, Blair. Blair! Put her down!"

I could hear Margie, but I ignored her. "Mick are you sure you see me? Can you hear me?"

Mick squeaked. "I can see you and hear you, Blair. You're scaring me..."

Margie grabbed my arm and I looked at her. "Can you see me, too, Margie? Can you hear me, Margie?"

Margie grabbed Mick by the belt. Her legs dangled from the ground.

"Then hear this from me. God is dead. He fucked up. He... She...It...is fucking dead. He never once has shown up to do any fucking thing but fuck it all up. Do you hear me? Do you hear me? How loud do I have to scream before someone fucking listens to me?"

I let Mick go and she dropped to the ground and I spat on it. "He fucked up. And Margie, neither you nor Mick here nor anyone can convince me that the fucking up doesn't fucking continue into fucking fuckdom."

Margie hissed at me, "What about Emma?"

Mom and Dad came to the front of my bungalow.

Fannie and the women from the rec center stopped their digging. "What about Emma?" I spat again.

"Is she a part of fuckdom?" Margie blurted at me.

I growled at all of them as if I were channeling Maya Angelou or old dead Gretchen or old dead Patches. "Leave her out of this." I opened my car door.

"No, Blair. I'm not leaving her out of this. Queendom fucking come or not. Listen to me you little marmie jackass. You've been beating yourself up since we were smoking cigarettes and getting high in junior high school. No one cares how you feel about your feelings. No one really cares about anything but themselves, really. Get off your pity pot and allow yourself to feel that something greater exists than you and your dumbass life."

"Fuck you, Margie. My fucking brother just died and this is how you talk to me?" I climbed in and slammed the car door. "You and the midget can leave town and never come back. What kind of friend are you?" I started the car and put it into gear.

As I sped away, Margie yelled. "I'm the best friend you'll ever have or lose!"

CHAPTER SIXTEEN

I was shaky and numb but the courthouse felt like home. When I accidentally stepped on some Indian Paintbrush flowers next to the state's flagpole Ray White stopped me and asked me if I was okay. I simply looked at him and said, "Aaron is dead."

He nodded and let me walk away. Fuck you. Leave me alone.

After the first recess, I talked to Judd and got up to speed as to what was happening. The letters were gone. Fannie had certainly handled that...evidently they'd burned along with the Mystic. Good work, Fannie. It sounded like the case was not far from closing arguments but there was one more witness.

Mr. and Mrs. Martinez were at their usual post and the reporters were all clamoring about when the bailiff did the "all rise" crap and Judge Archer entered the room. I took my post by the jurors and watched the court reporter look over her notes. When the courtroom was seated, Emma called another witness on behalf of Mary Louise Martinez.

Jack Palonski, husband to Millie. The air in the courtroom was like a galaxy of a million inhaling molecules of perspiration and desperation. Taut and tight.

I felt sick to my stomach as I watched a very short, gaunt Jack Palonski walk down the aisle in wrinkled khakis and a black tie on a white short-sleeve shirt. Even I knew that it was goobery.

Once sworn in, Jack Palonski sat down and smoothed out his thinning black hair. He smacked on a piece of chewing gum until he was quietly asked to remove it by the bailiff.

Emma, in a dark blue skirt and silk white top, approached him and smiled. "Mr. Palonski. Will you please tell us to whom you are married."

"Everyone knows I've been married to Millie for nearly fifteen years now."

He smiled and jerked slightly.

"Thank you. Now, Jack, may I call you that?"

"Yes."

"Now, Jack. Can you tell me a little about your marriage to Millie?"

"Objection." Virgil got on his feet. "Your Honor. This question is vague…what do we mean by a little?"

"I'm sorry, Your Honor. I didn't mean to intend anything little about the marriage between Jack and Millie Palonski," Emma said this and the courtroom erupted in laughter.

Bang. Down went the hammer. "Counsel, let's get a little more specific with your question. I mean just more specific." The courtroom laughed again. I had no room for laughter.

"Jack, were you present at the Sunday gatherings at your house over the years when players were allowed to come by and watch football and eat pizza?"

"Yes. I was present," he stated and looked at the jury and then the judge.

Emma walked toward the jury and near me. I looked at the floor. "You were present. And during these past few seasons, did you ever remember Mary Louise Martinez coming over?"

"No, I don't recall her being there."

"You're stating under oath that she never once came over, stopped by for a soda, had a chinwag with you or your wife at your home?"

"I know who comes to my house and who doesn't," he said with irritation.

"Jack, do you and your wife write notes to each other?"

"Objection—"

"Sustained. Counsel what're you doing?" Archer asked.

"Your Honor, if you'll allow me to establish this line of questioning, I think it will please the court to know where I'm going."

He shut his eyes. "Different question, Counsel."

She paused. The courtroom was still. Two reporters stopped taking notes and glanced up in Emma's direction. I cut my eyes her way too. What was she going to ask? I didn't know what she was doing, either.

"Jack. You love your wife, right?"

"Most certainly do. Yes." He nodded and folded his hands around the microphone. "Yes, we were college sweethearts." A beat and a pause.

"You met in college?" she asked.

"Yes." He unfolded his hands and looked at the judge.

"What college did you attend?" Emma looked at her notes. Mr. and Mrs. Martinez stared a hole into Jack.

"We went to Brigham Young University," he said and then offered, "She was in education and I was in business."

"So, you're both Mormon, I assume?" Emma glanced up.

"Yes, we are."

"Jack, do you like homosexuals?"

"I love homosexuals. Jesus tells us we must love all sinners. Do you love homosexuals, Ms. Jacobs?"

Emma laughed. "I most certainly do. Whether they're sinners or not is not up to me to decide."

My stomach twisted and I felt the sudden urge to text Margie and apologize but knew it would be the wrong thing to do.

"What is your general view on homosexuals, Jack?"

"I don't have one, Ms. Jacobs."

"Well, you did just tell me that you loved them, didn't you?" she asked and walked toward the witness stand and then turned to the courtroom.

"Yes," he said a bit demurely. "I love them, but I don't condone their behavior."

"So, what you're saying," she turned around to face him, "is that it's okay to be gay but you, as the Catholics might say, don't condone the sexual behavior?"

"Yes. It's in the Bible. Front and center...no doubt."

"Where?"

"Where what?"

"Where in the Bible?" Emma asked.

"You know. It's there," he said and then put his hand under his chin and flicked his beard at her and everyone. Ooo whee, I thought.

"No, I don't know. Bailiff...can you hand me your Bible?"

Todd grabbed the swear-in Bible and handed it to Emma. "Thank you, Todd."

She walked to the jury. "Now, Jack. You're Mormon, right?"

"Yes, we said this already."

"You've studied the Bible, right?"

"Yes. I most certainly have," he lied. My skin started to itch. I loosened my collar.

Emma smiled. "Then for me and the court and the life of Mary Louise Martinez. Please show us in here where it says you can't lie with a woman...you can't lie with a man...you can't lie with the best of them. Show me."

He took the Bible from her. Instead of opening it, he raised it up. "I don't know where it is specifically. But I know it's in here. It's an abominable sin. Loathing. Disgusting. Terrible."

Here comes Fred Phelps, I thought. Church of the Latter Day InSaints.

"So, Jack." Emma grabbed the Bible back. "You're saying that you agree that homosexuals are bad, terrible people who deserve to die."

"Objection!" Virgil nearly cleared his seat. "Your Honor, she's putting words in his mouth."

No one needed to do anything at all. Jack Palonski did it

for the LGBT world of bullying, blasphemy and crime. "That's exactly right, you slick little lawyer. They do. They should all be deported to the Middle East where they know what to do with them. Hang 'em...hang 'em!" He gritted his teeth, exhaled and shook his finger at her and everyone in the courtroom.

No one breathed for about five seconds. I could not believe what Jack Palonski had just said.

"And, ladies and gentleman of the jury, that's exactly what Mary Louise Martinez did. No further questions, Your Honor." Emma sat down.

Virgil, not willing to dig the hole any deeper, declined cross-examination.

Judge Archer told Jack Palonski to step down and he was taken to the witness room by Oneida.

To me and the rest of the LGBT world, it seemed like a closed case at this point. No love letters needed. This testimony alone from Coach Palonski's husband would sway any jury. But if there was a reasonable doubt, as evidenced by the suicide note, then the Martinez family was screwed like the way a bunch of high school Proposition 8 haters had shown up from California to ensure that homos were homos. Irritating as Fannie scratching her scraggily fingernails down my screen door. Emma had gotten to Jack. This was good.

The day before Aaron's memorial service, the emails and Twitters and texts were flying because the case was down to closing arguments. Mom pressed my uniform and Dad came by and brought more doughnuts. It was nice to see them get along but I didn't say a word about it and grumbled along. I left Stephen Hawking's part of the house untouched. Mick and Margie were on their way back to California. I'd texted her that I was a terrible person, a terrible friend, and thanked her and Mick. She did not respond. The thickness of Aaron's death and my disgusting behavior with Mick and Margie upset me.

Before court, I stopped to speak with Fannie and Diana, who were both out by the new gardens planting morning glories, impatiens, sweet alyssum, petunias, purple mountain grass, some vinca and others I could not name.

"What else are you going to plant?" I asked dumbly, picking up a pot.

Fannie took it from my hand. "You. You. How about that?"

"How about just my brother? I'll bring his ashes to you tonight, Diana," I said. Maya came bounding up to me and jumped up on me. I patted her on the head. "Good girl."

Diana was on her knees digging in the dirt. "Sounds good, Blair. It's going to be simple. Don't worry."

"Just tone down the God stuff, Diana. It wasn't him and it isn't me."

"Like that's a big swirling banner over my head." She smiled and got up and patted Maya on the head. "Good girl. Get the deputy dirty. You need to let go of the not letting go, Blair. Everyone who cares about you and Aaron, even your parents, really don't give a rat's ass about what you do or don't believe in. We're sick of hearing it. Or, not hearing it. Go on to court. Emma will be looking for you."

"You burned those letters up in the Mystic, didn't you Fannie?" I asked.

Fannie picked up two young rose bushes and plopped one in a hole she had dug. "I did no such thing. The fire was an accident."

"I'm talking about the letters you took from the courthouse. The ones written between Mary Louise Martinez and Millie Palonski."

Diana stopped and glared at the two of us. "The head fire marshal in charge ruled the fire here an accident, Blair. A candle—my candle. I accidentally hit it while doing a Tarot reading for Mr. Sweet and it tore up the curtains before we could even barely get out of there."

"Well good grief. Fannie...where are the letters then?" I asked.

"I don't know what you're talking about, Blair," Fannie said.

"Fannie." I patted Maya again. "Do you remember fifteen years ago when you told me to stay away from Emma? You yelled at me right next to this outbuilding while Margie and I were smoking cigarettes. What was that for?"

One rose bush was in and Fannie grabbed the other one. "The parents didn't need to hear them. It was an accident. I just felt like they didn't need to hear what was in the letters."

"You know now, Fannie, I'm going to have to arrest you for stealing evidence. If you tell me where it is, then I'll ask the judge to go easy on you…" But before I could get the rest out, Maya Angelou started to bark and then lick Fannie. It seemed odd.

Diana came in close. "If you arrest her, you know it's over between you and Emma." She winked and then acted like she hadn't said it.

It was true.

Holy Sophie's choice.

I thought for a second. "Well maybe, if you know the content of the letters, we can run you to court this a.m. and you can testify on the Martinezes' behalf."

Knowing who she was to the core, Fannie stood up. "The judge and jury will not trust me—the town crazy. It'll ruin Emma's case. You know that. Come here, Maya. Help me plant this other rose bush."

She was right. The letters were the only way. "Then tell me where the letters are, Fannie."

"They're right here," Fannie said after a moment.

"Where right here?" I asked.

Diana smiled. She knew too.

"All here—" She outstretched her flabby arms across the brief expanse of grass and garden. And then Fannie patted Maya on the head.

"Oh Lord, you planted them under the flowers? Really? Under all these flowers? Fannie, Diana. Please tell me you didn't plant the letters under the flowers?"

Just then, from her pocket, Fannie pulled out the last of the letters, how many, I did not know, and planted it firmly under the last rose bush she was putting in the ground with Maya's help.

Diana came up to me and hugged me. "You don't understand

Fannie, Blair. No one does. She's smart, intuitive, crazy, telepathic, schizoid…you name it. But, the one thing you and I both understand is, she's got a big heart. They were love letters. Private. This garden is for love. Aaron would have liked that. Those letters weren't meant for the courtroom, or *Oprah*, or CNN or the *Today Show*. They were private. Left in a shoebox in the back of a girl's closet where she could pull them out from time to time and remember."

"Did Millie write her back?" I asked. "Did she say anything that would corroborate the testimony we've already heard?"

Just then, an eagle flew overhead. We both looked up.

"Does it matter?" Diana said. "Mary Louise Martinez is dead. I hope between her and Aaron they can find a way to this…" And she put her hand to the crown of my head and the other hand to my heart.

I placed my hand on her hand and embraced Diana for the first time in a long time.

Fannie came from behind and yelled as loud as she could possibly yell, "Because I knew one day you would want to kiss her and I didn't know if I liked that idea or not but now I'm okay with it!"

She slapped me on the back and went toward my bungalow where my mom was drinking coffee on the front porch. I watched Fannie go into my bungalow and Maya walk to the doorway, to the screen to wait for her to come out. When she did, she gave Maya an entire doughnut and sat next to my mother with a mug in her dirty, grimy, filthy hand.

Jesus Christ.

Off to the courthouse, I drove by the hospital and tried to call Margie. I knew she was mad and I did not know if I could repair things or not. But, God, I was trying. Come on. Direct my sail whoever you are. Help me. Help Emma. Help Mary Louise's soul.

Oneida was chatting with a member of the HRC when I walked up the steps to the courthouse. The session was to start at nine o'clock and I still wanted to check some emails before I went in. Nothing from Margie, so I wrote her one instead.

Dear Margie,

I was out of my mind and heart and soul...please tell Mick I am sorry. If you will still be my friend, I will try to make up for the mess I've made. Will you come back and bring the midget and Ann and Nancy if you see them or perhaps...

I'm off to court...closing arguments. I hope Emma does well. I'm sure you will see the TV coverage.

Forgive me? I know it sounds a little Jesusy...but, I'm trying.

Blair Underwear

"Hey there..." a voice from overhead said. "How are you?" Emma touched my elbow and my knees drew in softly together.

"I'm fine. You should be with the Martinez family. What are you doing here?"

"Can we kiss?" Emma asked and put her leather folio on the desk next to mine.

I leaned back in my chair. "Emma, I think I may be arrested if we kiss in here?"

"You're funny. Were you writing me a love letter on your computer?"

"I think we're all out of love letters in this town," I said.

"I'm not so sure." She smiled and leaned down toward me and kissed me on the nose, then the mouth.

I pulled back. "My God...was it you?"

"What?"

"Did you take those letters?" I asked in a panic. "Tell me you didn't take the letters from evidence, Emma."

"Blair...now what on earth made you think that? I'm the purest girl you've ever met." She smiled and winked and leaned in again.

I pulled back. "Emma...are you and your mother and the gyrating gypsy into some sort of conspiracy here?"

"I've got to go, Blair. I just wanted to check on you. Maybe after this trial we can spend some more time together."

"I would like that, Emma. I really would." I watched her walk out. "Good luck today. I'm hoping for you."

She waved from behind. "Hope is a four-letter word, Blair."

Stunning.

And stunning she was in court.

"Fact," she addressed the jury. "Mary Louise Martinez was a star player on the Teton County High School girls' basketball team. Fact: She played under the guidance and tutelage of Coach Millie Palonski. Fact: There were both signs overt and covert that upheld the beliefs and ideas that no alcohol, no drugs, and no lesbians were allowed in the locker room of Teton High School. No lesbians allowed. How would you feel if no Jews were allowed? No Christians were allowed? No Muslims? No Hindus or Buddhists? No heterosexuals were allowed? No African Americans allowed? The fact is that the teachers, the principal the public school system all failed Mary Louise Martinez. They failed to take away the signs. They failed to look into the eyes of Coach Palonski and say, 'No, we will not stand for this kind of policy in our gym, in our classroom, on the court or any playing field.' The school is supposed to protect students from sexual harassment and bullying. Teens all over this country—every year—are harangued, harassed and humiliated into believing that what they think and feel—what they think and feel—is wrong. It's all over Facebook, it's all over YouTube, it's all over the social media, and it's all over for LGBT youth like Mary Louise Martinez. You, the jury, must know that she did not commit suicide by jumping off the ski lift at Snow King Mountain. She did not commit suicide by taking alcohol and drugs and locking her door and crawling into her bed. She did not commit suicide by shooting herself in Cache Creek Canyon. She did do it in the one place where she fell in love—the one place that betrayed her with a kiss: Teton High School's gymnasium. She hanged herself—just like Jack Palonski wanted her. A straight man who can tell you all about the Sodomites if he could only find it in the place where it is in the Bible. Please stop listening to the

Christian Right—the people who say they love homosexuals but then create the very atmosphere to hate homosexuals by being the catalysts for hate, for silence and for shame. Let's send the world a message. Stop. Stop. Stop the insanity and madness of beliefs that kill. The note is enough evidence to submit this verdict as guilty, guilty, guilty for hanging a girl who never made it to her nineteenth birthday. She never made it. So, let's find it in our hearts to give some small measure of justice and restitution to her parents and brothers and sister for this unimaginable loss, this tragedy. Find it in your heart, today, now! Now is the time. Not yesterday, not at some point in the future after more of this kind of calamity occurs. Right now. Thank you."

Virgil stood up and came forth with a deep silence, austere and brusque. Judge Archer opened his eyes long enough to watch Emma take a seat. Oneida caught my eye and I looked away.

In his snakeskin boots, Virgil leaned against the jury box and said nothing for what seemed to me like five minutes.

He cleared his throat. "Now, let's see. Fact: Mary Louise Martinez was a troubled teen who took her own life. Fact: Mary Louise Martinez was a young, talented basketball player. Fact: No evidence to date shows that the Teton County school system acted with any impropriety. We heard testimony from witnesses claiming that Mary Louise Martinez was acting erratically during the time before her death. Could it be that she made advances toward her coach? We don't know. We don't have any evidence that shows there was a relationship between the two of them. Both Millie Palonski and Jack Palonski have spoken of their loving marriage. Seems straight to me. As far as signs go, we know this. Teton County put its anti-bullying measures into place last year and that included, let me repeat, included, sexual orientation. Teachers had training, including Coach Palonski. The resource officer made a simple mistake almost two years ago. But she was the one who handled the anti-bullying training. Hell, even a GSA, a Gay-Straight Alliance, started this past year to prove that Teton County was behind the gays and the straights, if you will. Ladies and gentleman of the jury, this is a clear case of love that was unrequited. Mary Louise Martinez hanged herself in that gym because she was delusional—delusional about her sexuality? Maybe. If you recall in her suicide note...she was talking of angels and God and whispering in people's ears and giving Matthew Shepard a high-five or something when she got to heaven. Come on, people. She was sick in the head. Anyone who takes his or her own life is sick. They need help. Teton County Schools can't be the Prozac to a student's life twenty-four seven. This happened on a weekend. It happened in the school's gym. But Teton County is in no way to blame. The blame, if on anything, is on the parents. They should have known their daughter better. They should have been asking questions at the dinner table. They should have been the ones to notice a change in their daughter's behavior. This isn't about bullying. It's about bad parenting. Case closed."

The Martinezes looked pale, shaken, stricken. Virgil sat down. Judge Archer opened his eyes and read the jury its instructions and opined that it was now all up to them.

Once the jury was out of the courtroom, Emma went straight over to the defense team and shook Virgil Steele's hand.

CHAPTER SEVENTEEN

I don't know about alternate lives or other dimensions or heaven and hell. Or if the sadistic OCD-like behaviors in God exist or not.

It is not up to me.

Cogito ergo sum—I think therefore I am. Now, I was done with the thinking.

Once when I was eight or nine, I found a hunting knife that my father used for fishing and lay down on the couch when no one was home. I raised the hunting knife to just two inches above my stomach and a voice inside my head said *do it*. Something deep within the chasm of my very being was telling me to plunge the knife deep in my stomach—this life isn't worth it. For an hour in my small life, I let the knife hover over me. My fate was in my hands. Would I do this life or not? Even at that inconsequential time, it was the right thing to do: check out, forget about it. It will all be torture.

Now, as I sat at the edge of the flower garden behind the Mystic Market, I realized it was what was inside of me that was the baffling, bedeviling evil formed in the guise of an unconscious mind, an unconscious being, an unconscious soul. My worst enemy wasn't the knife, nor the torment of a thousand ills on earth. My torture, of course, was me. My own voice, small and insignificant. My own mind.

In my black buttoned-down shirt, I watched the mouth of Father Mark say a few lines about Aaron Wingfield. He said he was a great man. He said he was a good writer and poker player. He said above all that he was a great friend to the town, a great brother to me. For a moment, I wondered if Aaron could hear. For a second, in between the mumblings of the priest and my own breath, I swore I could hear the clicking of a keyboard and the Hawking voice come out saying: "Stop. With. All. Of. This. Glitterati. Go. Home. Smoke. Drink. Listen. To. Earth. Wind. And. Fire." I mused at my musing. I miss you, *Brochacho*. You were my best man. You were my hero. You were my testament to life. I'm glad to have stayed. If not, I would have missed you.

Emma put her hand on my back and I turned around and hugged her.

"Don't let go, Emma," I cried.

"I won't, Blair. I promise."

"You smell like honeysuckle."

"I do?" she asked.

Maya came from behind Fannie and Diana and Todd and Marty and had a flowered twig in her mouth. She dropped it at our feet and wagged her tail. I bent over and picked it up. It was one of the roses that Fannie had planted, dirt clod ball at the bottom, a letter attached.

Emma patted Maya on the head. "Good girl with a large name," she whispered.

"Yeah, she's no poet, though." We quietly laughed at that.

"What would Aaron want right now?" Emma whispered.

"I think he would want us to go to an island and drink drinks with tiny umbrellas," I said and handed Emma the dirty rose.

"Why, you're so charming," she said then pulled the note away and kissed it then put it in her pocket. "I'll have to bury this evidence later myself."

Just then, Father Mark did his ashes to ashes thing and set Aaron's urn on the table in front of him and unscrewed the top. My mom and dad and then Father Mark all walked down to the waters of Cache Creek and set my brother free.

It took twenty minutes for the entire service. When it was over, I walked from the crowds as I did not want to talk with anyone but the one I was guessing was my new girlfriend.

Back at the threshold of my small bungalow, Emma got a text.

"The jury's come back with a verdict."

Great timing. "I'm not changing," I said.

"Who would want you to?" Emma texted a reply to the court and talked at the same time.

"I mean my clothes, Emma—duh."

"Oh, come on, put that uniform on and come to the courthouse. Aaron wouldn't want you to miss this for the world. Nor would I."

I had to fight my way into the courtroom through the crush of the media and townspeople.

"All rise." We all did. Everyone in the courtroom was pin drop silent.

"Hear ye, hear ye, the General District Court of Teton County is now in session. The Honorable Judge Archer presiding. All those having pains or suit to prosecute speak now or forever hold your peace. May God save this honorable court. Be seated please."

The judge sat down and stated: "Ladies and gentlemen of the jury, have you reached a verdict?"

The tall mustachioed foreman stood. "We have, Your Honor."

The bailiff nodded and went to the jury box. The foreman handed the written verdict to the bailiff. Archer read it.

"Will the defendant please rise," Judge Archer stated matter-of-factly.

The faceless superintendent stood as did the faceless principal and Virgil. Archer handed the verdict to the clerk of the court.

Mr. and Mrs. Martinez, instead of looking at the faces of the jurors for clues, as most people would, stared at Virgil, their faces distorted by anguish and a baleful fury that could have burned a hole through his rumpled suit jacket. Mrs. Martinez clutched her rosary in white fingers.

The clerk then looked down and read, "We, the jury, find the defendant in the case of *Martinez vs. Teton County School District*—guilty."

Their faces transformed by triumph, the rosary dropping to the floor, Mary Louise's mother and father shot up like cannon balls and hugged each other. And then Emma.

I, frankly, couldn't believe it. A small family had beaten the system. The courtroom was bedlam.

Holy Atticus Finch. I was astounded.

The coutroom drama took on epic twenty-first century proportions just like the tectonic plates had clashed rock against rock a million years ago to form the purple mountain majesty just beyond Highway 22: The Grand Tetons. The civil case went right into the mystic against the backdrop of a case that was too loose, lacking testimony and garnering national attention many thought it did not deserve. It came out as surreal as it had begun: a basketball hoop, a death by suicide, a gnarled rainbow flag and a deputy sheriff who had witnessed the drama of a lifetime unfurl in the cataclysmic atmosphere. They should not have won, but sometimes truth and fiction surprised the hell out of all of us.

"Order, order!" Judge Archer shouted and banged his gavel. The energy was palpable and Emma was still hugging Mrs. Martinez.

Finally, a semblance of order was restored. The clerk continued. "We, the jury, find restitution in the case to the Martinez family in the amount of four point two million dollars." No one could hear the rest of what the clerk said. It didn't matter.

Four point two million dollars: a small price for a priceless life that once helped a old crazy lady in a moment of shame at a corner drugstore in Jackson Hole, Wyoming.

After the judge issued his standard message of thanks to the jury and concluded proceedings, the courtroom was still a bustle and I helped the jury out through the door to the jury room and to their respective freedoms now that their own ordeal was over. I caught the eye of Carleen Proust and she sneered at me. I sneered back and felt very good about it. I wondered if she was the one juror they had to convince to the Martinez side. My gut told me so and I left it at that.

The courtroom emptied to a media meltdown and Emma spoke to reporters as did Virgil. The Right was on Virgil's side, but I noticed something very interesting. The biggest crowd hovered over by Emma. Emma was the story. She always had been as far back as I could remember—ancient almost. I smiled and stayed in the background near an old oak tree and watched her give her small "the cause of justice won" speech to the crowd and to the Martinez family.

"Mrs. Martinez would like to say a few words to the press..." Emma said and shifted backward.

Mrs. Martinez approached the podium of mics. Her countenance appeared lined and tired but she smiled for a moment as she spoke in an Hispanic quiver. "My daughter was, eh, very beautiful." A hush came across the crowd. "My daughter was a loving, dear, sweet young lady. She was a star on the basketball court. Grandy and I watched her all these years...drove her to all her, eh, off-season games." She paused and inhaled and her husband put his head on her shoulder. "She was a good student. If she was a lesbian or not it did not matter to us but we never talked about it. Eh, we never talked about anything LGTB in our home." She got the acronym mixed up but that was okay. "We just did not know. This flag..." She raised the rainbow flag. "Eh, this flag was wrapped around my daughter's neck. It silenced her forever. But," she stumbled over her words, "my little girl is not silenced forever...instead she speaks to the world and says simply, 'peace.'" She held up her fingers in a peace sign and so did her husband. The crowd applauded and there were a few cheers.

Emma came back for a few more questions and finally thanked the reporters and the sheriff's department.

A woman came up from behind me, sinewy and smelling of cinnamon and patchouli. "She was one of the most talented basketball players I ever coached," she whispered under her breath. I turned to see a young woman in what looked like a Jane Lynch *Glee* outfit standing right behind me except she had on a ice-blue Columbia hoodie.

"Who are you?" I asked.

"My name is Piper Cliff. I was Mary Louise Martinez's AAU coach the past two summers up in Canada. She was an amazing player. I couldn't stay away from this…I'm horrified this all happened."

"Nice to meet you. I'm Blair Wingfield and that's Emma Jacobs up there. The Martinezes' attorney. My girlfriend." Emma looked like a goddess, perhaps Demeter. The pomegranates of her great trial emblazoned all over her.

"She nailed it. Didn't she?" Piper noted.

"Just like Jesus, I guess," I said.

"It feels good to nail it. This is a victory we all needed."

"Amen," I said.

"Awomen," she laughed and I laughed.

Piper shuffled her feet and stood in front of me. "Nice to meet you. I'm headed back home. Tell Emma, nice job."

And with that, her old coach was gone.

It took about an hour and a half for everyone to disperse. I was tired and wanted to be home with Mom and Dad in my bungalow.

My phone buzzed. I looked down to it and opened the message from Margie. "*No worries, Underwear. I love you. Water under the bridge…or a thumb in the dyke. See you soon.*"

God, she was disgusting but I chuckled anyway.

CHAPTER EIGHTEEN

I prayed.

I prayed in my head, I prayed in my bungalow and I prayed on duty. I prayed that Diana and Fannie would get the Mystic Market up and running again soon so we could all get back to our boring lives in a small inconsequential tourist town.

Emma had to go out of town after the trial because *The View, Joy Behar, Rachel Maddow* and all the morning shows wanted to talk to her about the trial. With Diana and Fannie, I watched her on TV and we all cheered her on. After about a week or so, she returned to her life in Jackson. She returned to me.

When she texted me for the gazillionth time that she wanted to see me and spend the night, I had nothing but goofy things to say like: *I don't know if I have enough room. There's nothing to eat. There's not a lock on my door. You might cuff me up when I'm not looking.* I was secretly afraid to have sex with an ex-straight attorney and told her so. She said that she would have to appeal to my senses to see what happened. When she used words like *appeal*, it made me quiver.

Maya Angelou scratched on my door the Saturday that Emma returned. I had taken Mom to the airport and we'd exchanged pleasantries and I love yous and we'll see you soons. My, we were a contradiction. Wasn't everything?

I let Maya in and scratched her chin. She licked my feet and my arms and kissed me on the mouth. Good girl. *Good to see you, my friend.*

"So, do you believe in God yet?" a very hot attorney said from behind my screen door.

"I'm learning to pray. I think I'm about halfway there. I've just never had any proof, evidence or data that God exists when all this other crap is going on. Come in, you hero!"

Emma came in and grabbed my hand as she sat down. "I'm whipped. Did you see Joy Behar? I love that woman. She's behind us more than we're behind us."

"So you're sure you're gay?" I asked.

"I was doing the straight thing for my mom. I thought that's what she wanted. Evan was a pathological asshole. I'd had girl feelings before him but repressed them because I thought she wanted babies and I didn't want to disappoint her." She crossed her muscled legs.

"Disappointing parents. We children are good at that aren't we? And they, as well, to us. Suddenly, I sound like I'm some old sage," I said.

"You are, dummy." She revealed her even white teeth in a smile.

I shifted in my seat and turned to Emma. "I bought you some Cheerios for our celebratory dinner."

"Wow, let the woo-dom begin." She smiled.

I got up and grabbed the box from the shelf. "I think you like Honey Nut, right?"

"Correct. I will stipulate to this."

I opened the box and gave a handful to Maya Angelou first. A hawk landed outside my window to regard my bungalow. Then,

I popped a Cheerio in Emma's mouth and then popped one in mine. Three robins fluttered about my screen.

She laughed and slapped her thighs. "Well, I'm full. What do we do now?"

I gave one more to the dog, one more to Emma, and one more to me. Slowly, I reached to Emma's face and cupped her head with my hands like they were their own chalices to hold the porcelain skin of her pure face. Emma leaned into my face and cupped mine similarly. Maya nosed out of my screen door and let me and Emma be. Being. A good word.

The world was still.

It was new and fresh and good. Love on my lips fell and pressed against the love on her lips as souls of a thousand years met again and joyfully regained presence—presence to fluidity, presence to cellular expansion, presence to time and space and now! I pushed Emma over and lay on top of her kissing and kissing and kissing. My tongue went in to hers, her tongue went into mine. Our legs intertwined. I pushed my hips into her hips and she pushed her hips into my hips, slowly, nothing fast. I moaned. She pulled away slightly, then breathed and moaned into my mouth. We parted then clasped back together in an inextricable passion that lifted our bodies to a height I'd never thought mine would go to or feel. My body lit up like the flaming Mystic Market and so did hers.

Once in my bedroom, it took us 2.9 seconds to take our clothes off.

"Lay down here, please," Emma stated softly. "Put your arms out and spread your legs, please, or I will cuff you up."

I did as commanded and giggled too. "Yes, ma'am. But are you sure you know what you are doing?"

"What, sleeping with a girl?"

"Emma, you know what I mean."

She laughed. "Oh, that. Well, trust me. Do you trust me?"

"Yes."

She sidled next to my outstretched body and suddenly I started to cry. Emma rose onto one shoulder and kissed me. "What's wrong?"

"All I can see is Mary Louise Martinez hanging in that gym.

All I can see are those kids from last year shooting themselves and hanging themselves and jumping off bridges. I can't get them or her image out of my mind!"

"Blair. Easy. It's okay. Think of the image if you can as one of redemption...like when Christ was on the cross. Think of it as transformation. Not of death but as transformation. She's not gone, Blair. She's here in all of us now." Emma placed her hands on my chest over my heart. "She took her life in an image that will burn in all of us forever...much like Christ. Much like any martyr does. All the children who've committed suicide because of the hate—they're all martyrs, sweetie, they're all birds."

"Emma?"

"What, Blair?"

"Thank you," I said.

Then Emma kissed me and released me all at once and she did so slowly and methodically as one might carve a figure into soapstone. She lingered above me, floated above me, she kissed my hair, my face, my lips, my forehead. Then did it all over again. I thought I would melt into my bed. Everything was soaked. My lips, my nipples, the red swollen ridges between my legs. It was an extraordinary ache in ordinary time. But there was no sense of time...this was all here and now. Emma's body on top of mine, our sweat commingled into a new sweat that rolled in its pearls down my side and onto my white sheets. She kissed every inch of me from my head to my toes. We laughed and laughed and laughed. Snot came out of my nose and she had to pull the sheet from the side and wipe it.

When she kissed me with her warm lips on my throat, I almost convulsed into the wanted spasms between my legs. A brief sight into the rapture.

When she slid her tongue all the way down in between my legs—the source of all pain and pleasure in women—I thought I would die.

But, all I did was come. And when I did, I said, "Oh, God."

My redemption was wholly complete—this time, in this life—finally.

We made love all night and most of the next day, then we went to the gardens and the place where Aaron had entered into Cache Creek.

Diana came from around the outbuilding with Maya Angelou. Maya wore a yellow life jacket. Diana had on her bathing suit and Fannie, egads, emerged with hers on as well.

"Oh, God, you're going to blind me!" I yelled.

"You-all go get your shorts on!" Fannie yelled. "We're going tubing down Cache Creek. First one down gets to have free ice cream on me and Diana."

"Let's do it!" Emma yelled and threw her hands in the air like she'd scored a touchdown.

And, of course, she had.

Fifteen minutes later, we all got into tubes. I donned my old Amelia Earhart hat for old times' sake and Aaron's cross around my neck. Maya was lying on a tube tied behind Diana. Down the ripples we went into the ceaseless summer evening, all borne into the present.

I looked up to the sky and as I held Emma's hand I yelled, "Fly, Aaron, fly... Go Mary Louise, go!"

Pray.

Peace...in the stillness of the day. Peace...in the stillness of the night. Peace...in the stillness of our hearts.

I prayed and prayed and prayed like my hands were around a rosary in a court of law.

Always and forever.

Awomen.

**Publications from
Bella Books, Inc.
Women. Books. Even Better Together.
P.O. Box 10543
Tallahassee, FL 32302
Phone: 800-729-4992
www.bellabooks.com**

CALM BEFORE THE STORM by Peggy J. Herring. Colonel Marcel Robicheaux doesn't tell and so far no one official has asked, but the amorous pursuit by Jordan McGowen has her worried for both her career and her honor.
978-0-9677753-1-9

THE WILD ONE by Lyn Denison. Rachel Weston is busy keeping home and head together after the death of her husband. Her kids need her and what she doesn't need is the confusion that Quinn Farrelly creates in her body and heart.
978-0-9677753-4-0

LESSONS IN MURDER by Claire McNab. There's a corpse in the school with a neat hole in the head and a Black & Decker drill alongside. Which teacher should Inspector Carol Ashton suspect? Unfortunately, the alluring Sybil Quade is at the top of the list. First in this highly lauded series.
978-1-931513-65-4

WHEN AN ECHO RETURNS by Linda Kay Silva. The bayou where Echo Branson found her sanity has been swept clean by a hurricane—or at least they thought. Then an evil washed up by the storm comes looking for them all, one-by-one. Second in series.
978-1-59493-225-0

DEADLY INTERSECTIONS by Ann Roberts. Everyone is lying, including her own father and her girlfriend. Leaving matters to the professionals is supposed to be easier! Third in series with *PAID IN FULL* and *WHITE OFFERINGS*.
978-1-59493-224-3

SUBSTITUTE FOR LOVE by Karin Kallmaker. No substitutes, ever again! But then Holly's heart, body and soul are captured by Reyna... Reyna with no last name and a secret life that hides a terrible bargain, one written in family blood.
978-1-931513-62-3

MAKING UP FOR LOST TIME by Karin Kallmaker. Take one Next Home Network Star and add one Little White Lie to equal mayhem in little Mendocino and a recipe for sizzling romance. This lighthearted, steamy story is a feast for the senses in a kitchen that is way too hot.
978-1-931513-61-6

2ND FIDDLE by Kate Calloway. Cassidy James's first case left her with a broken heart. At least this new case is fighting the good fight, and she can throw all her passion and energy into it.
978-1-59493-200-7

HUNTING THE WITCH by Ellen Hart. The woman she loves — used to love — offers her help, and Jane Lawless finds it hard to say no. She needs TLC for recent injuries and who better than a doctor? But Julia's jittery demeanor awakens Jane's curiosity. And Jane has never been able to resist a mystery. #9 in series and Lammy-winner.
978-1-59493-206-9

FAÇADES by Alex Marcoux. Everything Anastasia ever wanted — she has it. Sidney is the woman who helped her get it. But keeping it will require a price — the unnamed passion that simmers between them.
978-1-59493-239-7

ELENA UNDONE by Nicole Conn. The risks. The passion. The devastating choices. The ultimate rewards. Nicole Conn rocked the lesbian cinema world with *Claire of the Moon* and has rocked it again with *Elena Undone*. This is the book that tells it all...
978-1-59493-254-0

WHISPERS IN THE WIND by Frankie J. Jones. It began as a camping trip, then a simple hike. Dixon Hayes and Elizabeth Colter uncover an intriguing cave on their hike, changing their world, perhaps irrevocably.
978-1-59493-037-9

WEDDING BELL BLUES by Julia Watts. She'll do anything to save what's left of her family. Anything. It didn't seem like a bad plan...at first. Hailed by readers as Lammy-winner Julia Watts' funniest novel.
978-1-59493-199-4

WILDFIRE by Lynn James. From the moment botanist Dévon McKinney meets ranger Elaine Thomas the chemistry is undeniable. Sharing—and protecting—a mountain for the length of their short assignments leads to unexpected passion in this sizzling romance by newcomer Lynn James.
978-1-59493-191-8

LEAVING L.A. by Kate Christie. Eleanor Chapin is on the way to the rest of her life when Tessa Flanagan offers her a lucrative summer job caring for Tessa's daughter Laya. It's only temporary and everyone expects Eleanor to be leaving L.A...
978-1-59493-221-2

SOMETHING TO BELIEVE by Robbi McCoy. When Lauren and Cassie meet on a once-in-a-lifetime river journey through China their feelings are innocent...at first. Ten years later, nothing—and everything—has changed. From Golden Crown winner Robbi McCoy.
978-1-59493-214-4

DEVIL'S ROCK by Gerri Hill. Deputy Andrea Sullivan and Agent Cameron Ross vow to bring a killer to justice. The killer has other plans. Gerri Hill pens another intriguing blend of mystery and romance in this page-turning thriller.
978-1-59493-218-2

SHADOW POINT by Amy Briant. Madison McPeake has just been not-quite fired, told her brother is dead and discovered she has to pick up a five-year old niece she's never met. After she makes it to Shadow Point it seems like someone—or something —doesn't want her to leave. Romance sizzles in this ghost story from Amy Briant.
978-1-59493-216-8

JUKEBOX by Gina Daggett. Debutantes in love. With each other. Two young women chafe at the constraints of parents and society with a friendship that could be more, if they can break free. Gina Daggett is best known as "Lipstick" of the columnist duo Lipstick & Dipstick.
978-1-59493-212-0

BLIND BET by Tracey Richardson. The stakes are high when Ellen Turcotte and Courtney Langford meet at the blackjack tables. Lady Luck has been smiling on Courtney but Ellen is a wild card she may not be able to handle.
978-1-59493-211-3